DIPLO
POUNDS
& Other Stories

About the Author

Ama Ata Aidoo

Ama Ata Aidoo's literary career dates from when, as an undergraduate, she wrote her first play, *The Dilemma Of A Ghost* (1964), which was subsequently produced and published. She followed that up with *Anowa* (drama 1970). Since then, she has published novels, including *Changes* (1991), volumes of poetry and short stories including *An Angry Letter In January & Other Poems* (1992) and *The Girl Who Can & Other Stories* (1997). Her third collection of short stories *Diplomatic Pounds & Other Stories*, is due out in the first quarter of 2012. She also edited the widely-acclaimed *African Love Stories Anthology*, published by Ayebia Clarke Publishing Limited (Oxford, UK, 2006). Her books for children include *Birds & Other Poems* (2002). Aidoo has taught at colleges and universities in Ghana and the United States including the University of Cape Coast and Brown University. She currently lives in Ghana and is the Executive Director of Mbaasem, a foundation to promote the work of Ghanaian and African women writers.

DIPLOMATIC POUNDS
& Other Stories

Ama Ata Aidoo

ayebia

An Adinkra symbol meaning
Ntesie Matemasie
A symbol of knowledge and wisdom

Copyright © 2012 Ayebia Clarke Publishing Limited
Copyright © 2012 *Diplomatic Pounds & Other Stories* by Ama Ata Aidoo

First published in 2012 by Ayebia Clarke Publishing Limited
7 Syringa Walk
Banbury OX16 1FR
Oxfordshire
UK
www.ayebia.co.uk

ISBN 978-0-9562401-9-4

Distributed outside Africa, Europe and the United Kingdom
and exclusively in the USA by
Lynne Rienner Publishers, Inc
1800 30th Street, Suite 314
Boulder, CO 80301
USA
www.rienner.com

Distributed in the UK and Europe by TURNAROUND Publisher Services
at www.turnaround-uk.com

Co-published and distributed in Ghana with the Centre for Intellectual Renewal
56 Ringway Estate, Osu, Accra, Ghana.
www.cir.com

British Library Cataloguing-in-Publication Data
Cover Design by Claire Gaukrodger
Typeset by FiSH Books, Enfield, Middlesex, UK.
Printed and bound in Great Britain by CPI-Cox & Wyman Ltd., Reading, Berkshire

Available from www.ayebia.co.uk or email info@ayebia.co.uk
Distributed in Africa, Europe, UK by TURNAROUND
at www.turnaround-uk.com

Distributed in Southern Africa by Book Promotions (PTY) Cape Town
a subsidiary of Jonathan Ball Publishers in South Africa.
For orders contact: orders@bookpro.co.za

The Publisher wishes to acknowledge the support of Arts Council SE Funding

Contents

Acknowledgements

I would like to acknowledge the generous support of the following friends, colleagues and organisations in the course of putting together this collection: Amina Mama and the African Gender Institute (AGI), Bisi Adeleyi-Fayemi and the African Women's Development Fund (AWDF), Rose Mensah-Kutin and Abantu for Development and Korkor Amarteifio and the Ghana Denmark Cultural Fund and Nana Ayebia Clarke, my publisher, for so much else.

New Lessons

I was getting ready to settle down. So out came the novel I am currently reading, the morning paper, the book of crossword puzzles and my Sudoku. I smiled to myself for the usual silliness in piling all that by me when I know that normally, at least for a good hour after I arrive, I just sit and do nothing...

I have always blessed that wonderful benefactor in my heart since I started coming here. On behalf of the other inmates as well as for myself: as a retired and rather tired professional woman, looking for wider spaces with which to shrink my day-to-day world. And if that sounds like a contradiction and a confession, well, it's both. I do have a cozy apartment which I nevertheless get regular urges to escape from. But then I also don't always feel like going to mingle with glorious humanity at the supermarket or the department stores or my otherwise treasured neighbourhood café. Or at the cinema. And let's face it: as for my friends and former university colleagues, they are all a bit like me. Not wanting to be in anyone's face is not considered a crime.

By the way, don't ever believe anyone who says that you

can run but you cannot hide. Actually, you can run and you can also hide. In fact, hiding is the easier part. It's running that is often quite difficult. After a certain stage and time, running gets downright impossible. I should know. Hiding was always easy. It has even gotten easier. With access to the internet and the mobile phone, you can hide very well and forever. These days, you cannot only choose where to hide, but for how long and how completely. And all with more precision than before. For some of us, this realisation is exhilarating beyond belief.

I am hiding. I am in hiding. You want to know who from? Everybody. Meaning that amorphous humanity known as my relatives. If you are interested, then please use your imagination and break that up into its possible parts. You also want to know where from? Home. It was the last visit that did it. It began at the airport. Mind you, there was nothing wrong with the airport per se. Rather, it was everyone else that was coming there from the city and the rest of the country. Awful! Awful! Awful!

I knew something was funny as soon as I unfastened my seatbelt, picked up my handbag and dragged my hand luggage to the exit. What first hit my face with the force of a blow from a giant's fist was the heat. But that I'm used to, or should be by now. Except that as I descended the stairs, I became aware with each step that I was getting enveloped into, or swallowed by ... something. Something quite unpleasant and alien. Something like solid air. Thick and clammy. With a sweet unsettling scent. Like clean and perfumed death ... That's it.

I hadn't been home in a decade.

From the tarmac, through immigration, to the carousel to collect my two pieces of luggage, down the long ramp and through the security exit, out through the last door to meet my welcoming crew of cousins and nieces, then into the waiting car, that thing into which I was sinking never went away. Or faded. Or dissolved. Indeed, what was dissolving was me. And I have since admitted that one of the great miracles of my entire life is surviving long enough at home this time around to return here. Of course, I am never going back there. Never.

'But Auntie,' chimed Princess, the boldest of my nieces and my favourite, when I was going on and on about before I left the country this last time, 'you never wanted to live here anyway. So who should have organised this society for you along more healthy lines?'

'You see ... ,' I tried to respond to her.

'I see what, Auntie? And now if, as you've been insist-ing, once you leave this time around you are never coming back, then who is going to get this country out of the mess for you?...Eh, Auntie?'

Ugh. That hurt. Not just because it came from her in particular. But also because I knew that she knew that not only do I insist on staying permanently abroad with infre-quent visits home, but my children, her cousins, have never ever gone home. Over the years, I never managed to make my country seem like an attractive place for either of my two daughters or my son to visit. And as a place to live and work? Forget it. Now, everything is worse down there of course. So much worse than it ever was.

3

But then at my age, what can I do about anything, beyond returning home like a good old African elephant to die? Actually, I won't even do that. I would rather spare them the need to deal with one more death. One more corpse to freeze, thaw, wash, dry, oil, shower in pomade and douse in perfume, dress up, *lay in state(!)*, then proceed by word, deed and song to flatter, appease and worship and if necessary, give it a change of clothes within a twelve-hour period for no other reason than that the rest of society should know that the family can afford it. No, I'm just never going back there.

It had to be a single donor. Such a complete and wholesome gifting. And maybe as a symbol of deep understanding. A gesture that had to have been made by an individual. If the donor was a man, he must have added to that special pool of human misery that is the product of abuse and then later wanted to contribute something to its management, and of course shut up an otherwise rowdy conscience. Or it was a woman, who had been, yes, a victim? What a truly nasty word – and when she had been rescued, or when she had rescued herself from the horror of it, had wanted 'to do something about it however small' to blunt a pain, or a memory of pain. I don't know any of the facts.

But it had to be one benefactor, not several. This space could not have been acquired with the dribble drabble of fundraising efforts. No way. The building is a lovingly designed fortress set in the middle of a vast estate. So incredibly green in the summer, with preserved clumps of ancient oak trees and pines, modern shrubberies of exotic

4

plants and pretty flowers. The lawns too are so well tended you know that the bequest must have come with careful instructions for the property's maintenance. In winter the snow shrouds it in a lonely and mysterious beauty. Of course, I avoid the place then because of the cold. But I have researched and learned that it is a sanctuary of sorts. An oasis. The great quiet outside gives me the right to imagine that there is some desired and welcome stillness within its walls. In fact, I have long admitted to myself that I regard the place almost as holy ground, then I chide myself for my new and unnecessary sentimentality. But maybe, sentimentality is the sort of thing that comes with retirement and old age...

Now what do we have here? Two cars have come into view. First, a maroon symbol of stylish but careful money. It is followed at a discreet distance by a black, self-consciously fashionable but useful petrol-guzzling sports utility vehicle. A young woman gets out of the first car, locks its doors and approaches the front of the building with the confident stride of a resident. Now a man pulls into the driveway in the second car, gets out of the vehicle, does not lock it... Did he forget to? Or is he in too much of a hurry? He follows her with the peculiar manner and gait of those who know what they are doing but are not too clear about why they are doing it: kind of hurriedly but hesitantly at the same time. When she rings the bell the gate opens from within. She goes through it and disappears into the building. The man stands still for some minutes watching her go, then he moves as if he too would ring the bell. He pauses however, and rather returns to his car. He does not get into the car immediately but stands by it for a while, looking absolutely pleased with himself, though also rather lost in thought, as if planning his next move.

That's when it occurs to me that the man is following the young woman who has just walked into the building. In *following her* – not for himself, but clearly for someone else. He is a paid agent. The thought does not startle or even surprise me the slightest. After all, I've been around and about long enough to know that such goings on happen all the time, all over the world.

But look, he is finally getting back into his vehicle. He moves away, very slowly at first: as if he is trying to get the car to think with him. Now I can hear him revving his engine. Then he speeds out as though he can't get away fast enough. I scold myself for being a nosy somebody. After all, I come to relax and avail myself of the peace that is here. Not to spy on spies.

I found this place by accident one day when I was indulging myself in the luxury of just driving around. When I saw it, I knew that it was exactly what I would have looked for, if I'd been actively looking for anything. I come here at least once a month in the summer and much of the rest of the year except in the winter proper. Yet I've never got used to the idea of a place that is so near a busy city but which is so completely secluded. And wonder-of-all-wonders: so absolutely still that I have figured out what it is from the way women of various ages come in and go out of the building. They are all clearly much younger than me. The traffic is often in groups of

6

three or four, but occasionally singly, and always carefully – you could say furtively, they get into cars and drive away. Then when they return, they almost run out of the cars and rush indoors. They never sit outside in spite of the beauty of the surroundings, the arbors, the comfortable benches positioned here and there, with planned randomness. I have also noticed that I am invariably the only one around. To begin with I feared that one day someone would accost me, inquire of my business and then send me packing. But so far, no one has. When any of the residents emerge they either ignore me completely, or sometimes acknowledge me with a diffident greeting…

He has returned. He has got out of his car and is striding purposefully towards the door. He's quite close to it. He is stretching out his hand to ring the bell. He has paused… And now he's hurried back to his car. He opens the door but doesn't get in. He has left the door open and is pacing about. He seems oblivious to my presence. Now, at last, he returns to his car. This time he is getting in. He drives away.

This second appearance has confirmed my earlier suspicion. I was right all along. He is a spy. Possibly paid by the woman's man: husband, lover, whoever. So he returns. He should, if he is any good at his job. No, I'm not bothered by the thought. My only regret is that I did not take a good look at his quarry. As for me, old or not, I'm still a woman, and despite years as a notoriously rigid academic and fierce critic, I want an old-fashioned and romantically happy ending to this story. At least for her.

That's why I am actively wishing him ill with a nicely rounded female curse: that he falls hopelessly in love with that young woman, whoever she is. That would complicate things very nicely for him, wouldn't it?

And in the meantime, what I've got to admit is that whoever first said 'nowhere cool' knew exactly what they were talking about. After all, much of the time, most of the places where we are likely to live on this earth are either hot, very hot, or cold, very cold. And cold ain't cool.

No Nuts

There's nothing on this earth quite as handsome as us in mourning. Black on black? Cool. So we love funerals. Half of the time, we don't even know who is dead, but we will be there anyway. No. That's not fair. We would know the deceased of course. He could be my aunt's husband's uncle on his father's side, or my best friend's best friend's brother-in-law or some such remote connection. But we shall be there and should be there.

We would have to be there, at that funeral. The men trailing in yards of *adinkra*. Black. Dark red. Midnight blue. Some colours that could only be created here and nowhere else. Colour like burnt blood. Or a mixture of dark blue and red and grey. Also brown. Like dead leaves under giant trees in ancient forests. Burnished gold. All metallic. These days, it's the men who are wearing the jewels: rings on their fingers, thin gold chains around their necks, hair close-cropped. *Ei*, our men can look so handsome. The women in the latest but more modest black *printex* or *shadda*. Or if they are of the *boujie-boujie* crowd, then of course, it's your voile, or lace or even silk.

9

The *kaba* cut in the most fashionable and most out-rageous styles, the *dukuu* sitting with studied roguishness on the pile of a huge coiffure.

You too, did you have to ask if all that was her own hair?

From the church we accompany the dead to the cemetery, while relishing being alive ourselves and beautiful. We put them in the grave, the priests do more sermonising. We throw handfuls of earth on the coffin, which makes a sound like none other actually. Then we go back to the house of mourning, where, if they have remembered to provide the ritual pots of water, we proceed first to wash the cemetery off our hands, and then move on to the next major business of the day, which is serious jollification. And even if they have not provided any water, *hei*, who cares about all those old-fashioned customs anyway? We still move on to the real business of the day. We sing. We dance. We drink. We eat. Then we go back to our homes to wait for the next funeral.

Except that here and now, it hurts like nobody's business to lose a friend like No Nuts. Dear Lord, the pain. Pain that has nowhere to go. Pain that breathes and moves like a pregnancy. Yet if I tried to talk about it, people will be clear about this too. They will have some advice for me. That I don't have to work myself into a serious headache about her death, because death is waiting out there for all of us and in any case, she was only my friend. That we were not born out of the same womb. We didn't even share a clan totem, and on and on. And on …

I know that for every human death, there is usually one person who is inconsolable: someone who feels the death so keenly, her heart truly breaks. What I am also learning is that that mourner can be a lover or a husband, a wife, a child, a parent. She or he doesn't have to be a family member. She or he doesn't have to be known to anyone close to the dead. But she mourns. He weeps. In fact if there were blood behind our tears, such people would weep blood too. I, Jennifer Nana Aba Amosiwa Cobbold, I am such a mourner today. That's why everyone has gone away, but I'm still here at her graveside. Nobody knows what I'm going through. Nobody.

No Nuts had to be special even in death. Apart from me, there are two other people whose spirits are completely broken because she is gone. One is her uncle the architect, and the other is her little sister, Korkor, who is out there somewhere trying to be a model. Those two are suffering more than the rest of the family. They don't know that I know. But I do.

... So probably, those two know that I too am suffering?

....

Mariama, thank you for coming to take me home last night. With so many people around, I was hoping, but fearing too, that someone would notice I was missing. So thank you. I could easily have slept all night at the cemetery and if I had, something quite terrible might have happened to me. You saved my life. In return as I promised, I shall talk to you as I have never talked about

11

No Nuts to anyone else, and never will again after this afternoon.

What did you say you wanted to know?

Everything?

Ah, my sister, I am not sure I can tell you everything. No, not even you.

Why not?

Because, I am not sure of what 'everything' in this case means. In fact, I wonder what everything is, when it comes to me and No Nuts.

About only her?

Okay. I shall try to tell you what I know ... You see how we are missing her already? She was the storyteller among us all. Mariama, you know that I was always a listener, not a talker. So now, the only way you can get me to talk is if you ask me questions so I can give what answers I can.

No, you were not alone in wondering where the nickname came from. We knew that other people did too. But we were not about to tell. Not to Rose, you Mariama, Ten Ten or Sister. And if we did not tell you people, then you must have known that we were not about to tell anybody else. Not even her mother. Anytime her mother asked us about it, No Nuts and I just looked at one another and giggled. Like a pair of schoolgirls. Of course, we knew that everyone suspected it had something to do with some man, evenings out, having a good time. And, in a way, that wasn't far from the truth. After all, everything that had to do with No Nuts had to have some man in it somewhere... And evenings out... And, r-i-g-h-t! Having a good time. Everytime. *Abi*? That was my sister, my friend. That was *Monua Basia*. That was her and her life.

Now listen. The name No Nuts came from something some guy had said one afternoon in London...

Yiw, Lon...don.

Mariama, are you going to keep quiet and listen to me?

You see, after we finished at Nkwaso Secondary School...

Yes, we were in school together...You didn't know that? We were.

Actually that's not why we were so close... Mariama, how many questions do you think I can answer at once, eh?!... My Sister, please let me deal with one question at a time. I shall come back to No Nuts and the education story... Maybe another time. What I was saying is that after secondary school, we never met here again. Then years later, we bumped into one another on some street out there in London.

Yes, just like that. It was from that time that we started being friends. Proper friends.

My brother had taken us to a party and introduced us as 'my sister and her friend.' Just those simple facts. His sister and her friend. As though we had no names. When this Englishman shook her hand, he looked at her as if she was a ghost: something he had never seen the like of before. Like a vision of the Virgin Mary. The Holy Mother herself. He stared so hard at her that it became embarrassing. Especially because he looked too handsome himself. Like a film star. Around us, people stopped whatever they were doing and stared too. Then she asked him why. He just opened his mouth and told her that her skin was pure chocolate. 'Smooth milk chocolate, with no nuts in it at all.' We all laughed. He turned red. For the rest of the afternoon, he kept completely to himself, just drinking beer after beer after beer and stealing glances at her, while other women, black and white, stole glances at him, hoping desperately to catch his attention. We didn't know when he left the party. But No Nuts and I knew he would try and get in touch later. He did. He turned out to belong to some fancy class. You know the English and their classes?! Anyway, it was clear that from that one encounter, he had made up his mind to marry her and keep her in England.

You are right, Mariama. Trust our sister to hook a real big fish and then let it go! But no, she won't have any of it. When I teased her about him, she told me that when she was leaving home, she hadn't told her people that she would return with a white husband.

Yes, Mariama, I agree with you. That was a rather startling response from No Nuts. So in order to deal with my own feeling of discomfort at that kind of explanation for her lack of interest, I asked her this: whether before she left home she had promised her people that she would return with a black husband?

Ow, you are laughing, Mariama. But I was serious. Anyway, No Nuts just looked at me like she didn't know I could be so stupid. When I insisted on a response, she looked at me fully in the face and said quietly but seriously too: 'Amosiwa, it will be complicated.'

14

'How?' I had challenged.

'It will just be too complicated,' she insisted with rising irritation. So I let it drop. The name occurred around that time. It started with me teasing her by calling her 'pure chocolate.' When I did, she replied: 'No Nuts.' In the end, I just called her No Nuts.

At the end of our courses, we both returned home.

No, I don't know what happened to the Englishman. I doubt that she did either. But think of it. What kind of life would she have had if she'd stayed in touch with every man who brought his heart to her to break? Hmm?

Were all these rumours true then? How would I know? It depends on which ones you heard.

This one was true. Every man she laid those eyes of hers on fell in love with her. And so did his brothers and his cousins. It was ridiculous really. Too funny and beyond laughter. This one was more than true. Young men. Old men. Middle-aged men. From coal black men to white men who thought there had never been any black blood in their ancestry, and looked it. So why did she choose this rascal to fall in love with? 'Ordinary Looking Rascal.' Ha, ha, ha, ordinary looking rascal. You are like her father. Just as bad. He couldn't stand him. He called him 'that rascal.' And that had No Nuts boiling.

Yes, that is his name, Obo Tan.

No, I haven't forgotten that you'd asked me why, with all these men on their knees, she should have chosen this one. Mariama, you too. Do I know? How would I know? Am I her heart? Did she herself know? Listen, *Monua Basia* Mariama, the only thing I know is that in the end, she had loved only one man and as we all now know, for only a very short time. And it is the same one you and her father describe as a rascal. I can tell you something else too. You know how everyone had always said around here that love is death? Well, deep down, No Nuts believed it. She took it literally. She always talked and behaved as if, were she really to fall in love, she would die.

Yes, it's strange and sad, but that seems to be exactly what has happened.

Did you say 'so what?' So when she became aware of herself as a woman, like from her mid-teens, she took her heart out of her chest, wrapped it very neatly in cotton wool, put it in a nice jewelry box and locked it up in a safe place. Then from when she was sixteen years old until she was thirty-eight, she set about the very serious business of living.

But why was she so afraid of love?

Something tells me that she had seen and taken note of what happened to other people who really loved. Men and women. They died. Or she thought they did.

'Something always happens to those who love. Sometimes they really die. Feely-feely. For real. They do die and go into eternity. Or something they had which had been living dies. Their ambitions, if they had had any. Other hopes and aspirations. Maybe some simple faith in human goodness. Their laughter. Yes, their laughter. That is what vanishes first. Always.' She sounded old, bold, certain and wise all of a sudden.

'But only when they are not loved back,' I suggested timidly.

'Huh,' she laughed. 'And how many people who love deeply ever get loved back?' Of course that shut me up.

How is it that all this happened to her in the end then? How would I know? Am I God, as my grandmother would ask? Was I there when she was saying goodbye to her Creator? Mariama, I don't know how come all this happened. What I suspect is that one day, her heart just got fed up with the imprisonment. So it worked its way out of all that cotton wool, carefully pried out the lock of the jewelry case… or broke it open, breathed a little bit of fresh air, sighed, then crawled back home into her chest and settled down.

That is exactly what I am saying. I agree with you. Our hearts have minds of their own. They can definitely take their own decisions. Though they are awful at taking care of themselves, and us …

No, it couldn't have been the fault of No Nuts's heart that the first man she took notice of after it returned home was this 'ordinary rascal.' But that is life. That is destiny.

No, it's not true that she had fifteen houses scattered around this city. She had only eight. Six of them were built for her by three men. Actually, only one of the men built a house for her. Two in fact. And Mariama, maybe you will find it hard to believe but that was also the one man who had not lasted even a year in her life…

Of course, she was lucky… and didn't we always know that? The four other houses were built by the two men with whom she had her four children. The houses were for the kids: two for each set of children. She built the remaining two herself, including the one that became her home.

How could this Obo Tan build No Nuts a house, when he had no job and clearly earned nothing? In fact, No Nuts was building him a house…the only one which her uncle had not designed… No, she had not asked him to. She had not had the courage to ask him.

Don't look at me like that. It is the truth. And I hate myself for blurting it out just like that. Why? Because, if you don't know about that house, then I suspect that it was one of those secrets she shared only with me.

No, her parents wouldn't have known about the new house-building project. Her father smelled out that young man a long time ago, hadn't liked his scent, hadn't wanted to see him, hadn't wanted her to be near him and No Nuts was very aware of all that. In fact, every single member of her family and her clan hated him thoroughly and completely. Another long story. But it meant that everything about their relationship became a piece of confidential info she could not possibly share with too many people, including and especially members of her own family. And the house was quite high on her priority list. Of course, now that what has happened has happened, the family will learn about it. Definitely. Something about it will crop up.

Maybe in her will? Not likely. No Nuts has not made a will. She didn't think she had any business 'drawing up wills.' She believed that it is unlucky. She shared that one superstition with all of us here. 'Begging the fates to do their worst. Not the kind of thing a mother of young children should be doing. And me not even 40 years old!' Of course, now they are going to fight over her property and may God in His Kindness help her children.

Sure. I shall help her people to look after the children. If they let me. And if it becomes necessary... In fact, I think we should all get ready to help. But then, we may not be needed in the children's lives anyway. The men who fathered them are decent polygamists...

Are you laughing at the idea of 'decent polygamists?' Don't. I know it's what our English teacher used to call oxy-something or other. But I think there are some. Men who at least take care of their various children and other responsibilities...Yes, there are some decent polygamists. Anyway, it didn't matter what kind of a man one thought he was. Once he made the mistake of entering her world, No Nuts treated him the same as all the others: with her usual indifference. If she thought you could make a good father, you stayed a little longer. Of course, all of that changed, when she met Obo Tan.

What do you mean by 'from then-on?' 'From-Then-On' is where we are today. They became lovers. She was his *alomo*. He was her person. For a while No Nuts looked like Happiness. Her eyes danced. Her skin shone. She allowed herself to put on some weight.

You are right. We were all surprised. No Nuts? She who had always avoided rich foods? There she was, at ten in the morning of a Wednesday, still among her pillows, eating stewed chicken and *banku*.

Oh yes, from the same plate as 'that rascal.' And as she would confess to me later with a wicked smile on her lips, they would have been making love all night and all morning. After some time, things settled down. They always do, don't they? In any case, No Nuts had trained herself too well. She resumed her work habits. Then one day, while we were on our last trip to Hong Kong, she told me on the plane that she had missed her period.

I was not surprised. Not at all. What had seemed strange to me then was the cool and calm way in which she had broken the news to me. It was strange because, if I had not heard her say it a dozen times, I had definitely heard it twenty. 'Amosiwa,' she would say, getting all humble, 'I have always thanked God for my four children. Two girls and two boys. Such an ideal number and with the proper balance.'

Don't ask me. Ask her. Listen to me asking you to ask her what? I have forgotten that she is dead! Hmm ...

I know. The first time she said that to me, I nearly fainted and then almost cracked my ribs laughing, before I too asked her: whose 'ideal number?' Mariama, you will kill me. But you are right. She actually used that expression: 'ideal number.' I told her that in the old days, people would have begged a woman like her to have twelve children. So she should not break my ears with any 'ideal numbers'... Of course, being beautiful and intelligent everyone assumed that she would have passed on all that beauty and brains to every single one of those twelve children! And yes, everyone knew she had the means to take care of them, and more!

20

What did she say next? I'll tell you. All this time, she was laughing with real tears streaming down her cheeks. She calmed down a little to ask me if we are not thanking God that the old days are gone forever?

Don't ask me. Ask her. Oh, listen to me again. I'd forgotten that she is dead. Oh, life...

Mariama, I keep saying you will kill me. But you are right. Because, she then added that these days the IMF, the World Bank and everyone in the global village business would not mind if she had had only one child, or none at all. Ah, No Nuts. She was even special in the way she had of throwing such talk around.

Say that again. She was aware that she had been blessed. With great beauty, intelligence...

...And then wealth. And to top it all, four healthy children. 'Two girls, two boys... *Na mempe woeyi, na mepe den?!*' She would address all this to me, charmingly, as if I were the main auditorium of the National Theatre with a full house.

When she told me about missing her period, I also told her that that did not necessarily mean she was pregnant. She giggled and said that in all history, there has only been one woman who could be said to have been genuinely surprised to find herself pregnant and her name was not Lucinda Mena Esi Eshun.

Yes, that was her full name. You know that whenever she gave you all of it, you had better listen and listen well to whatever followed.

Listen, my frien', now that we are talking about these things, maybe we better talk? Don't you know that No

Nuts and I had heard about you people?

What do you mean, 'heard what?' We had heard that the four of you were jealous of the two of us!

Mariama, don't tell me that's not true. No Nuts and I were aware that you and Rose and Ten Ten and Sister were complaining that the two of us were always stuck together like two snails under dry forest leaves.

It's not 'old woman talk?' It's what you people were always saying! How was it that we were six friends, but the two of us were always going together? But you, Mariama, you know that although we were six, we were also in twos. Like you and Ten Ten and... Sister and Rose.

Oh no. We shouldn't fight. No, you are right. This is not the time for this kind of silliness.

Did she tell me she was going to keep the baby? Not exactly. Anytime I asked her, she told me that it was a long story.

You are right. Nothing used to be a long story with her. Our Madam will say it or not say it. 'Eat it or not... but make it quick,' she always insisted. That's why I began to think that maybe something was not quite right when she kept putting me off with: 'It's a long story.' It was strange meeting a confused No Nuts.

You want me to tell you everything I know? I thought I had already said that where No Nuts is concerned, I don't know exactly what 'everything' is? Okay. I shall tell you the little that I know. No, I shall not weep. No, we better not. After all, even if we wept as many tears as all the waters of the sea, she will still not come back. Never, never, never ... But bring your ears here. What is coming is all I can remember from our talk some evenings.

My sister, what I can remember and what I can tell you is really the same thing ... After all, you were her friend too. Besides, the woman is actually dead.

And buried. So what can I or anyone of us, or even any common stranger tell you that can hurt her now?

...Funny you are saying that. You also remember that, don't you? She cracking us up anytime we went to a funeral together, declaring that she had no problem *at all* with death? None. Apart from the fact that people didn't come back? So could she make one suggestion for its improvement if she were ever to be consulted by God? That people be allowed to come back, after a while, healed of their injuries or illnesses and diseases. And if it was old age that killed them, they should come back younger. Yes, her idea was that we would die a little, go away for a while to rest, get ourselves renewed and then come back. That was her Divine Highness's suggestion for improving on death ... Or life!

Ow, No Nuts. Ow, ow, No Nuts ∴ No Nuts.

Mariama, *daabi, daabi, daabi* ... I shall not weep again. As you and I know, she always referred to the current man in her life as her 'Person' ... No, I am not crying. I've told you I'm not going to cry again.

They got properly married. At least, all the traditional things were done. That was also when her people showed their dislike for him, this Obo Tan. Her architect uncle especially couldn't hide his contempt.

She obviously decided to marry Obo Tan soon after they met and that was the only time the architect openly disapproved of any decision she ever made and any action she had ever taken...Her father was no different. But this was also a time when, sadly, an outsider like me was not much help. All I could do was watch her defy all of them.

Yes, she did: solidly, clearly, publicly. She made it quite clear that she was having none of their objections to the relationship. The whole business was bad for everyone.

Don't you remember her telling us all about it? Mariama, you should remember why you and Rose and Ten Ten and Sister could not come for the ceremony. But I was definitely there for the occasion. It was not a happy one. No. They went through with it. They finished it. But you would have thought it was a funeral they were arranging and not a marriage.

You are right. Listen to what I too have just said. *O Nana Nyame...*

The only thing I came to know about No Nuts and her 'Person' was that towards the end, they had two different futures planned for the relationship. He thought they would have a big wedding after the baby was born, while she was actually planning to leave him altogether, the minute she returned home from the hospital with the baby.

How come I knew that? Simple. She had told me. 'Going to kick him out of my life' was how she put it.

That was true. If I don't remember that, then what will I ever remember? After all, we are talking about events that took place very recently. A few months ago. In fact just last month! Mariama, it is true. No Nuts told me that she was going to kick Obo Tan out of her life. 'Nana Amosiwa, *motwa n'boot*,' she swore. Now those beautiful legs that would have done the booting are rotting in the grave at Awudome. O Lord, did she have to die? Dear Lord, did she?

No, Mariama, we said we won't cry again.

How could she have been planning to dump the same man for whom she was building a house? I don't know the answer to that one. Nor do I know what he had done to make her come to such a drastic decision. And who knows, she probably didn't mean to do it. Just something she had dreamed up to get all those of us who were anxious about her to relax. Anyway, by the time she confirmed to me that she had missed her third period, I concluded that she was going to keep the baby anyway. What I had not suspected then was that No Nuts had already gone to see her doctor. Our doctor, actually.

Yes, we had the same gynaecologist. A very nice and sober gentleman who took excellent care of us through her four pregnancies and my three…

Ah, ah, ah, Mariama, is this the time not to be serious? If No Nuts and I had gone through other pregnancies that didn't end in babies, where did those other pregnancies go? Yes you heard me: four pregnancies for her, three for me. Don't let me hear you hint at anything like that again. You are a good Muslim girl! Shame on you. And didn't you know that both No Nuts and I are good Christian girls?! Shame, shame, shame! Go wash your mouth with soap. Naughty, naughty Mariama.

Hmm…you are right. Love is a dangerous project. Yet, what would we do, if we never loved? What on earth would we do? What kind of life would we have?

At the beginning, I was a little nervous about the doctor we had found. For two reasons. We had heard he was good and so we went to introduce ourselves to him. I knew from the very first day we went to him that in the end he too would burn for No Nuts. Yes, the doctor too. So I was afraid that he was going to find it difficult to take tough decisions about her health. Then listen to this. After we had actually gone together to see him, by ourselves, no one begging us to, we then became nervous that he would share the medical information on either of us with the other. Were we mad or what? But as it turned out we need not have worried. He was always strict and proper with her. And as for our medical information, we realised soon anyway, that any information we had not shared with one another already was not worth much: medical or not.

As I was saying, she had gone to see him after our last trip to Hong Kong. She said she had asked for a general check-up and a pregnancy test because by then, she was about nine weeks gone.

Yes, really.

Doctor Quoffie was very angry with her. He thought she had been irresponsible and he found a very nice way to tell her so. According to her, the rest of the interview went like this:

Doctor: 'Lucinda.'

No Nuts: 'Yes Doctor.'

Doctor: 'The lab result is in and it's positive.' No Nuts just looked at him, with that wicked smile dancing around her mouth. 'I remember you telling me that your last child was going to be your last. And that was about four years ago.'

No Nuts: 'Yes Doctor. This was a small accident.'

Doctor: 'A small accident! Listen, woman, by the time the baby is born you will be forty years old. That's risky.'

No Nuts (petulantly): 'But Doctor, I want it. I want this baby.'

Doctor: 'You want it? Why? What for? Didn't you tell me that you were divorcing your last husband?'

No Nuts: 'I divorced him.'

Doctor: 'Uh?'

No Nuts: 'I remarried.'

Doctor: 'You what?'

The Doctor could hardly contain his rage. But he also knew that he was only her physician. He had to be careful. He chose his next words cautiously, returning both of them to the confirmed pregnancy. After all, that was what she had come to see him about.

Doctor: 'But marrying again and having another baby are two different projects.'

No Nuts: 'My new husband doesn't have any children of his own. Not even one. He wants me to have this one for him.'

The doctor almost laughed out aloud. Of all the green reasons for having a baby and in her current situation, clearly putting her life on the line. He had been a gynaecologist for over twenty years. Women had always amazed him, especially with the reasons why they make babies. Nothing ever to do with themselves. It is always for others. Always. Or nearly always. Meanwhile he disagreed with those who insist that pregnancy is not an illness, because he considered it as a major attack on any woman's system. Colds and flus are illnesses. A pregnancy is much, much worse…

It occurred to the doctor that maybe this pregnancy was not really an accident, small or not. He chanced another question.

Doctor: 'Well, if he wanted children that much, why didn't he make some earlier?'

No Nuts: 'He told me that he had never really wanted to marry, or have children until he met me. And Doctor, he wants the children from me.'

Yes, Mariama, yes. No Nuts would have sung that one like a song.

Doctor: 'That I can understand.' The doctor had said that quietly and bitterly, almost to himself. More aloud, he added: 'Frankly, I still don't advise it. Forty is not too late to have a baby these days. But it is still risky. In this case because of the fibroids. Actually, you don't even need this child … and you are aware of that fact. Or should be.' After an uncomfortable pause during which neither of them spoke, he continued: 'Besides, you've gained a lot of weight in a short time…even this early, your blood pressure is higher than normal.'

No Nuts (According to her, she had insisted on being her stubborn self throughout the consultation): 'But Doctor, I really want to have this baby for my new husband.'

   The doctor had been aware that he had never before in his professional life had to struggle so hard to stay calm, cool and collected.

Doctor: 'Even at the risk to your own life?'

They both knew he had crossed the line.

As you know, part of No Nuts's charm was her ability never to raise her voice in any kind of argument.

No Nuts: 'But why should it be so risky? None of my pregnancies were difficult. And you always said that I delivered easily.'

29

Doctor: 'I agree. But think back. Earlier you
had no fibroids at all. And later, they were not
so well-developed. This time, it's different...
Quite different.'

At one time – it must have been her second child,
a girl – she had nearly given birth on a plane.
Of course, she had lied to our travel agent about
how far gone she was, when she went for her
ticket. Or rather, when the agent brought the
ticket to her house. She was then thirty-four years
old, or thereabouts. And although looking at her
now she seemed to be even younger, the doctor
knew that inside, her age would show. Like all
humans and all other animals.

Doctor: (Returning with some difficulty to the
present and to her, all the while completely
aware that he was being quite unprofessional,
considering how many other patients were
sitting outside his door. In any case, what would
she think, facing him and watching him so lost
in his thoughts? Anyway, picking up the
discussion, he had added hopelessly): 'You were
younger then.'

He had expected her to protest at the reference
to her age. She had not. There was only that
annoying smile still playing around her mouth.

No Nuts: 'Women are making babies in their
fifties these days.'

With that she had alerted him to the fact that she could not possibly have done so much world travelling without catching on to some of the relevant international debates about women's health and making babies. That, at least, she had allowed herself to show interest in those that affected her personally.

Doctor: 'Very true. But under very special circumstances.'

No Nuts: 'Then let's treat this as a very special circumstance,' she commanded.

Doctor: 'You will have to agree to come into hospital for the last month then.'

No Nuts: 'But Doctor...'

Doctor: 'You will have to.'

He had given that final order firmly, in an attempt to regain his authority. They both knew that the consultation was over. Then he had given her what must have been some appropriate prescription and asked her to try and be regular in the meantime with her monthly check-ups. She had left.

Mariama, I didn't know she had not returned to consult our doctor again. I don't know whether she had decided to transfer to another doctor. All I know is that she kept the pregnancy but, from a certain point, No Nuts just shut up about her condition – at least with me.

And beyond a certain point, we cannot pry into other people's affairs if they don't want us to. Not even with our closest friends, or relatives.

So yes, Mariama, I imagine that that was the last time Doctor Quoffie saw No Nuts. Until I called him in a panic at three o'clock in the morning six months later, knowing that if anybody in this city could save her, it would be him. When he entered the room, he swore. Then all of a sudden, he was an Olympic athlete, sprinting to her side. He took a long look at her and then examined her carefully. Then he turned to look at me. I knew at that moment that No Nuts and her baby were no more. I began to wail. He and the other doctors ordered me out. Later the death certificate indicated that the actual death had occurred only a minute after I had left.

Mariama, what do you mean by I should have done something earlier? What could I have done?

Diplomatic Pounds

Believe me, I wasn't aware that as some kind of a fool-proof solution to her weight problems, my poor Cecille had become something of a collector of bathroom scales: analogue, electronic and combinations of both. And frankly, that's what comes of not listening to me, her mother. I can still see us two girls in Abidjan, Rio, Prague and everywhere else they sent her father calmly chatting about this thing. As if we were not Africans. I would tell her: Cecille there is no answer. The only answer is not to eat. Look at me, I would command her. And when she was younger she would actually look at me before saying softly: 'I know, I know. Lady, I know.'

She and her brothers call me 'Lady.' Of course, they borrowed that name for me from my mother and other older relatives when they were growing up. From her mid-teens, any time I asked Cecille to look at me, she jumped up and started screaming that we were two different people. And she knew she could never be like me. When she hit her mid-twenties, and by the time she got married, she would still jump up and scream that we were two different people and all that. But then she had

33

graduated to adding that she didn't want to be like me anyway. What's the point of being in the diplomatic service if one isn't going to explore the foods of other people?

Ai, Cecille. It was my turn to scream. That this was not part of your father's mission: that he and his family carry the weight of his job on their person. Cecille, it's not even part of the cultural brief. And then look at it this way. This life is full of lunches, cocktails and dinners. Look at us in a place like London, I would command (that was when her father got one of the plums, the Court of St. James). I used to tell Cecille, darling, look at us here. If I've learnt anything as your father's wife, it's this. Apart from the UN in New York and Rome itself plus the Vatican, London has the most embassies in the world. Over one hundred, Cecille, over one hundred. How are we to cope if we eat our way through everyone's celebration days? Eh, Cecille? I finally gave up completely when she began to ask me what life would be worth if everyone behaved like me and ate nothing at all? And then being Africans, and with so much hunger on our continent, wasn't it sheer insensitive cheek that we had food but would not eat because we didn't want to get fat?!

Cecille owns bathroom scales from the early 1920s to tomorrow morning: wooden affairs with touches of antique elegance and rural charm; contemporary health-o-meters that measure weight, body fat, blood pressure, bone mass, just name it; and everything else in-between. Shocking, huh?! And they are everywhere in this house.

34

At least one in each of the three or four general bathrooms, and three in the couple's bathroom en suite. There's a pair of scales at the back of an unused drawer in the kitchen. There's a pair hidden under one of the two fake fringed European period chairs. And that's right here in the lounge. 'Louis Quatorze,' Cecille had declared with some triumph to me once when I commented on them. 'Louis Quatorze? Would those be fringed?' I had wondered to myself. After all, I am the family expert in these matters. I am Madame Ambassador. Even though my daughter doesn't seem to appreciate this, or any of my other unique gifts and experiences and accomplishments. My poor Cecille. In this house, there are bathroom scales inside wardrobes and by other clothes racks. There are scales behind every single door: upstairs, downstairs and in the basement too.

And for me, what is really shocking is discovering that each one of these monsters works perfectly. Can you imagine?

'Clearly, the only way Mrs. Wiggleton feels confident about her ability to monitor her weight is to have bathroom scales spring on her wherever she is at home… in her own house. So to speak. ' The psychiatrist said this wickedly and turned to me with an ugly wink as if to ask me to agree with him that Cecille has gone ga-ga. Can you imagine? His patient and my daughter? Where are his professional ethics? Don't psychiatrists take the oath of Socrates or whoever? Believe me: although the lighting in his office was not the best in the world (it might also have been my own poor eyes you know), I could have

35

sworn that after the wink, he kept a smirk on his face and I had to summon all my powers not to pick my handbag to wipe it off...'

'Am I wrong, Mrs. Wiggleton?' It took my Cecille about two full minutes to answer him. Can you imagine? She shouldn't have bothered at all.

'You are not wrong, doctor.' My poor daughter normally speaks with such a clear and confident ring. But she said this in such a tiny voice, it broke my heart to hear her.

'And that's what I am talking about.' Cecille continued, 'It's as if those scales had been reading my mind all this time. But my mother does not want to believe me. That when I woke up this morning, all the bathroom scales in my house had gotten together and formed some kind of a giant wall or barrier. They won't let me enter the kitchen.'

'At all?'

'At all, doctor.'

'Could you get to anywhere else?'

'Yes.'

'So it was only the kitchen you couldn't enter?'

'Only the kitchen... and doctor... sh... sh... don't tell anybody. Especially my mother.' And with me sitting right there? 'To make sure that I never ever miss an opportunity to weigh myself, I've put quite a bit of money into a couple of the new robotic bathroom scales. They are programmed to ring or beep anytime I get near them.'

Can you imagine? Very, very shocking. The robots will ring for only her to hear. Not her husband. Not her children. And definitely not me. After all, since this crisis,

I've been in her house walking around and not heard a thing. My poor darling child.

The doctor whistled. Then, 'extraordinary,' he whispered under his breath. I could not stand the thought of going to him in the first place. And that was just the idea. Even before I met him it occurred to me that he was secretly laughing at my Cecille. But her father thought we should. And you know how he is when he gets an idea into his head? Homeboy. So what? All that it means is that before you can say Gulf-of-Guinea, this business will be all over the place. We are high class. In fact, our family is the highest. After all, who else among our people here in London are ambassadorial retirees? Eh?

I admit that a few of them were in the Service too. I mean the Diplomatic Service. But none of them got to be ambassadors. Not really. And so they like to pull us down. People don't change because they now live here in London instead of Accra, Lagos, Freetown or Monrovia. In fact, they are worse here. Life is easier, so people have more time to gossip. They'll be whispering how the Ambassador's daughter has gone crazy. But Cecille has not gone crazy. She is just having a little nervous breakdown.

Did You Ever?!

Araba found herself wondering if there would be time for Koku to take them all the way home from the subway station before returning to his office. She very nearly suggested that maybe when they got to somewhere halfway, he could put them in a taxi... however, she did not voice this idea aloud. She thought that maybe he could let them do the rest of the journey home without him because, after all, they were back in a completely familiar landscape and she was not exactly a child. Then suddenly, it occurred to her that spending as much time with them as possible that afternoon might have less to do with protecting them from the streets of New York than providing evidence of how much he had missed them while they were away. So she experienced a kind of shocked delight – not to mention relief – when Koku himself suggested that he did just that; relief because he had bought her time. Time to get home and settle the boys in. Time also to settle herself back in and get ready to tell the whole story: properly.

So how come she was shaking with something like dread? Now that they had had supper, the boys were asleep and she and Koku were in their bedroom with the door shut, and he was saying: 'So Rabs, please tell me what it is?'

'My people don't like our children,' she replied quietly, simply.

'What?!' That was an explosion from him. Then a pause. 'Wait a minute,' he continued. 'What exactly did you just say?'

'I said that my mother and the rest of my family don't like our children.'

'And why not?'

'In fact, one of my aunts told me quite clearly that they wouldn't know what to do with two boys. They think they should have been girls. At least, one of them.' She said this in a whisper.

'Well, as you know, we are a matrilineal people.'

'Yes so?'

'That means that entitlement to land and other clan properties depends entirely on what your female line is...'

'Meaning what?'

'Meaning, who your mother is and her mother is or your great-great-grandmother on your mother's side was? That sort of thing?...' Araba responded.

'What?' Koku exclaimed again and again. Then he began to pace up and down the bedroom, not even aware that he was doing so in response to some mysterious law that insisted it was his turn to pace about.

After a moment, he started to laugh. Startled, Araba asked him what was funny? But her question only sent him off into more paroxysms. At intervals, he tried to calm down: but as soon as he made any attempt to speak, he just roared again. This went on for what seemed like a very long time but maybe it was not. You know how funny time can get…

Quite silly and unreasonable?…

So that nobody should tell anybody anything about time at anytime, anywhere and in any circumstance.

A minute that stretches itself into a day…

A year that collapses itself into a month…

And how about all those weeks which never seem to know whether they are coming or going?

After a while, Araba managed to get through to him. So he put his arm around her gently, and moved with her to sit close on the edge of the bed, with both their feet planted firmly on the rug.

'Why do you think my news is so funny?' she asked again. But this time with an impatience she could no longer hide. Although he had stopped laughing, he did not answer her right away, as though he felt that he had to weigh up carefully what he was about to say. Eventually he spoke. 'Because Rabs, as you already know, where I come from they only celebrate the birth of boys.'

This piece of information momentarily stunned her with its unpleasant familiarity. Araba had been aware, especially since secondary school days – rather vaguely though – that outside the boundaries of Akan lands were all these other people for whom girls were not only not worth much but, in fact, were often regarded as problems that demanded solutions; chaotic distractions that called for tight packaging and were ultimately, expensive non-luxuries. She did not know what to say at that moment and was not even sure that there would be any point to anything she could say.

In any case, Koku was talking, repeating himself, his voice rising slightly:

'...Yes, where I come from, girls don't matter. Nobody wants them. Only boys are desired, cherished.' Now he is shouting, his voice booming through the night. Quite clearly at this point, they have both forgotten that they might wake up the boys.

'I know... I know... I know.' Araba was saying this while feeling like her heart was shifting gears inside her chest.

By the way, which doctor said that our inner organs are not always where we think they are?

Here and now though, she found herself wondering what else could hurt so much if it was not her heart...

'Koku, it's not just your people,' she continued sooth-ingly, 'I know that's how it is in much of the world.' Her voice dipped further. 'Actually that's how it is almost everywhere else.' He whispered. They looked intently at one another and all they could see was extreme confusion in each other's eyes. Koku began talking again:

'When I phoned home to tell them about our first baby, that it was a boy, my father gave a huge yelp: that "God is great" and then he just left me on the line. Probably to run to tell my mother and the rest of the household. I could clearly hear my mother and the other women ululating and thanking God. It was the same the second time around; he left the line open so I could hear them. At the time I was very glad thinking they were just happy that I'd got children.' A very long pause. Then he continued: 'But in retrospect, I think it was because the kids are boys. Rabs, I'm now certain that if we had had girls my father would have sworn under his breath, and then stayed on the line on both occasions to console me with something like "God will be kinder to us next time."'

'Uh-huh?' Araba asked softly.

'Yes,' Koku responded miserably, then he added, 'as for my mother, she and the other women would have wailed openly.' Another long pause followed, during which Koku moved Araba into his arms as if trying to keep her from breaking up. Literally.

'Rabs, you are crying!' he exclaimed as much surprised as anyone could be, if greeted with the news that the Sahara desert had sprung a tropical rainforest overnight. His wife was not of the crying kind. She didn't say anything aloud in answer. But she agreed with him anyway.

*Yes, I am crying. But I am not crying for you my
husband who was born male in a place where boys
are 'cherished.' And I am not crying for me who was
born female among a people who treasure girls.
No, I am crying for all the girls who were ever born
where they are despised. I am crying for my boys,
our sons, and all the boys who were ever born where
no one really wanted them. My dear, I am crying
for our children. Koku, my dear, I am also crying for
a world in which nothing ever makes sense.*

That was only one year ago. This evening, and once
again, Araba and Koku are sitting on the edge of their
bed. Their kids are sleeping. Clutched in Koku's tight
embrace, again tears are streaming down the face of this
newly weepy Araba. This time, it's eight more weeks after
the confirmation of an unplanned pregnancy. She and
Koku have no intention of going for any ultrasound early
gender detection nonsense. They don't want to know.
What they know is that they are already so excited about
this baby, whatever gender it turns out to be. The
thought of a third child makes them feel like a pair of
naughty and silly teenagers. And they can't help giggling.
And Sissie, all this could make even a stone cry. But
Araba is not a stone but a woman born of a human
female after all. Just like her husband Koku…

Outfoxed

'I hadn't been home in some years. Not since my kids were born. And of course, I wanted to show them off to Mamaa...'

'Esaaba?!' exclaimed a decidedly shocked Awo.

'Uh-huh?'

'What did you just say?'

'That I wanted to show my children off to my mother?'

'Esaaba?!'

'Of course. No two ways about that.' Esaaba's voice was full of amused interest.

'You shouldn't talk like that.'

'Why not?'

'She's your mother.'

'So?'

'Esaaba, certain pieces of information are for sharing naturally with people like...'

'Our mothers?'

'Sure... sure... not because we want to annoy them, or irritate them, or ...'

'Or otherwise score points with them?' Esaaba asked

her best and only friend Awo, with a sneer that made the latter cringe. That's how come Awo paused before she could repeat her 'sure,' 'sure,' this time whispered.

'But then, that's only if they act like our mothers. Awo, Mamaa had never been exactly motherly with me,' Esaaba persisted defiantly.

Awo has to admit that she is not just shocked but also distressed. Her friend, this friend – she always had others besides Esaaba – had always seemed so cool, collected and reasonable. But this early evening, she is meeting a different Esaaba at what they both call their 'corner greasy spoon' by London's Piccadilly Station. Awo is not sure she wants the introduction. The friends often meet here for a quick cuppa and a scone each, before they part to join the rush-hour crowd, on their way to reconnect with their separate lives after a hard working day or very busy shopping on a Saturday.

A whining Esaaba? Awo finds herself concluding that 'all this' must be part of the aftermath of the Fall of the Berlin Wall, or 9/11, or The Great Tsunami that hit Asia and the East African Coast. Or the total effect of those and all the other incredible world disasters which she never ever wants to talk about, but which Esaaba is always wanting to drag up for discussion. And now, she remembers that every now and then, her friend had dropped a hint here and a hint there about how she and her mother were never the best of friends. That had disturbed Awo a little, since she and her mother really were more like an older and a younger sister than parent and child... This is so clearly different... In any case, her friend seems angrier than she'd ever noticed her to be about anything.

'Esaaba, I keep telling you, you should not feel like that.'

'And I keep hearing you.'

'She is your mother.'

'So how should I feel?'

'I don't know. But she is your mother.'

'And girl, do I know that!... Who else could be so close to me and know me well enough to hurt me that much?!'

'Ess, I am very sorry.'

'It's not your fault.'

'No, but I am still very sorry.'

At the end of her first year in secondary school, Esaaba's mother had had brief encounters with two different men around the same time. And after she found herself pregnant and could not or would not name which of them was the actual 'owner' of the pregnancy, her family had made sure she married the one they described as a 'Christian gentleman.'

'If you had not come along, who knows, but I might have gone to university... too.' Esaaba's mother had always insisted on having her daughter share this particular regret from when Esaaba was getting dressed for kindergarten, all through her childhood and into university. Whenever she became articulate enough, she would try to defend herself, and always in one sentence only. 'Mamaa, it's not my fault,' in response to which her mother would knock her on the head or pinch her hard on any part of the child's body that was closest to her.

47

'Petit bourgeois. That's my mother. Whoever coined the phrase must have thought of her. Very petty. Very bourgeois. A small-minded townswoman. An old-fashioned-know-all, who as a school teacher was convinced that it was her responsibility to beat education into her pupils and also solemnly believed that, as a parent, if you spared the rod, you most certainly spoiled the child.'

'Ah-h-h, Ess.'

'I realised quite early that tears did little to stop her. That in fact the more I screamed, the harder she caned me. So I made up my mind when I was about nine that I would never again respond to any of her beatings with my tears. Never.'

'Oh Ess.'

'I stopped myself from crying whenever she hit me. But that helped nothing. If anything, not crying made her mad, since she read my attitude correctly as defiance. In fact, that seemed to inspire her to keep on hitting me until she got tired. From then on, she always whipped me within an inch of my life.'

'Ei-i-i, Ess.'

'Then one day she stopped. I knew my plan had worked. It must have occurred to her that if I was not crying, then there was no way she could tell how badly she was hurting me. And since she was nobody's fool, it must have also occurred to her that if she was not careful, one day she would have a dead child on her hands.'

'Please, Ess?'

48

'What do you mean? You don't think I'm lying, do you?'

'Of course not. But it all sounds so cruel and horrible and should not have happened to you ... or ... or anyone's child.'

'Well, it happened to me.'

'And your own mother?'

'Yes. My own mother.'

'I am so sorry.'

'I keep telling you it's not your fault.'

'Mmm...'

'So stop apologising. Besides, there was also always the small matter of skin colour.'

'What do you mean?'

'The politics of it.'

'The politics of what?'

'Awo, are you listening? I mean the politics of skin colour.'

'What of it?'

'Awo, please pay attention. I am talking about how skin colour was a thing among the three female members of our nuclear family: Mamaa, our mother, my younger sister Ruby, and me.'

'Are you serious?'

'Dead!'

'Esaaba, I am so very sorry.'

'My sister, it's not your fault.'

'But for not getting it all this time you've been trying to tell me about it.'

'Even then, I was always only trying to. I never really told you about it, did I?'

'It all must have been so awful!'

'But I always knew that the only one for whom it was a big deal was our mother, whom I called "Mamaa" like all my siblings, but whom I secretly referred to as "that woman".'

....

'When I was my mother's only child, it was just the "if you had not come along, who knows blah, blah, blah..." bit. After my sister Ruby was born, it was also: "Heh! Ruby, you are fair... like me. Thank God. Because people can see you are my daughter. You resemble me. But as for you Esaaba, you look exactly like your father. Too black."'

'Oh no.'

And both mother and daughter would be very clear that the father referred to was not the husband and the father they lived with. Which later got the adult Esaaba always wondering how her mother had managed to sleep with her real father to conceive her, if his skin colour had revolted her that much... No, Mrs. Sarah Coleman could never ever be accused of being too subtle in any way and certainly not with anything that she considered negative about her oldest child and whoever this child's natural father had been.

Awo's head is pounding with confusion and horror. She has by now admitted to herself, if secretly, that this is the most difficult conversation she's ever had with her friend, or anyone for that matter. Ever.

'Maybe that's exactly why I wanted to show the kids off

to her,' Esaaba continues, almost recklessly, clear that she is absolutely right.

'Mmm...,' is all Awo can add.

It is still quite light outside, although it is much later than they would normally allow themselves to sit together and relax. But it is summer time and in this part of the world, daylight lingers on for much longer at such times. In fact, you sometimes get the feeling that the sun does not ever want to go away.

All this is several years after Esaaba had left home on a rather cool day in July to come to London for the first time. The big rains had just about petered out. The heat would hit in another day or two, but had not just yet. The morning of her departure, Mamaa opened the door to Esaaba's room without knocking and made herself comfortable. Esaaba had ignored her.

'Esaaba.' Mamaa had opened what she had mentally decided was going to be an important family discussion with a whisper that was full of 'we-girls-understand-one-another... or-should.' 'You know that I don't want to sound like one of these women who harass their daughters into marriage. But you also know that a woman is nothing unless she gets married: no matter what else she achieves in this life. You know that...' Esaaba had groaned audibly. The mother had not intended to pause and so pressed on.

'... You are telling me that you are going out there for your Masters, a second degree. But my child, I gave birth to you. So I know you. And knowing you, I suspect after that you'll go on for a third and may be even a fourth degree...' Esaaba could only stare at her mother in complete amazement. How could anyone who made a point of not getting them to be close also know her that much?

Mamaa had paused at that point, first to catch her breath and then secretly wonder at her own brilliance. She had looked up at Esaaba waiting for her to say something: either in agreement with her very accurate reading of her daughter, or maybe to get the daughter to contradict her. But Esaaba was too shocked to say anything...although she had been telling herself for some time that she would not allow anything her mother said, or did, to shock her again. In any case, she was too busy this time to attempt to react. Or so she told herself.

'Esaaba, are you really sure your mother said all those things... to you?'

'Yes, and that was not the first and would not be the last time. My mother would often say hurtful things like that to me and as regularly as she liked to and wanted to and thought she should or when the spirit moved her. So you tell me, my friend, my sister, how anybody can continue to think of any woman who treated her like that as a mother? As her mother? Does any woman live anywhere on this earth who is capable of dealing in this way with her own child, "her own bowel-begotten child"? As our old folks would put it?'

For a response, Awo could only stare at Esaaba. And not unlike the way Esaaba – for other reasons of course – had stared at her mother the day she was getting ready to fly out.

'Esaaba, don't look at me like that,' her mother had admonished. 'You don't have a teaspoonful of common sense in that head of yours. And all this education won't help. I am your mother, so if I don't try to get you to see the value of practical sense, who on this side of the earth would? Eh? And then what will become of you?... Eh?'

'But Mamaa, women getting Masters is so common these days ... and even Doctorates,' Esaaba said, packing as much fatigue and boredom as possible into her voice.

'Oh degrees are fine,' Mamaa had cut in, 'but go out there and also look for a husband for yourself. I beg you.'

....

Esaaba had just shaken her head and continued with her packing. After all, she had a plane to catch to London where she had lived for two years before meeting Paul and marrying him two years later. They had their first child, a boy, in another couple of years. He was followed at the end of eighteen months by a second child, a girl, who was around four years old when she took them with her on the trip back home.

A total of about eight glorious years away from Mamaa? Sheer bliss.

She had almost not married Paul out of sheer spite. Oh no, not for him. But of course, for her mother. She and Paul had been dating for two full years when he proposed and made it clear that he was not taking '"no" for an answer,' as he put it.

Having convinced himself of her deep respect and

53

affection for him, he had been somewhat perplexed by her persistent and unexplained refusal to consider marriage. But he had soldiered on until he finally wore down her resistance.

The first time Esaaba phoned to tell her mother about herself and Paul, Mamaa's response was: 'Esaaba, my own Esaaba, you've been reasonable for once and acted on my advice… And you say he is a white man? Ah, ah, ah, my sweetheart, if you were here, I would have carried you on my back!' And Esaaba was surprised to find herself making some appropriately giggly sounds, instead of vomiting on her handset, which is really what she had wanted to do. That was also the year Esaaba got her Masters. And contrary to her mother's fears, she decided to get a job instead of going on to enroll for her doctoral degree.

'I was not keen,' she told Awo. 'Like I said,' she continued, 'it had nothing to do with my feelings for Paul. In fact, to the extent that I could be in love with anybody,' and her friend couldn't help but wince at this point, 'I was very much in love with Paul. Still am … ,' she added, almost to convince herself. 'No,' she continued, 'I just didn't want my mother to feel that I had been "reasonable for once" and acted on her advice and congratulated herself. And of course, congratulate is exactly what she did once she got the news … because in actual fact, I'd been more than reasonable. I'd given her an extra excuse to preen, by marrying 'a proper white man.' Of course, I later tried to reason from that high by trying to convince her that white men are also just that:

men. But no-o-o, as far as she was concerned what would have been the point in living in a European country, if I'd not gone and caught one for myself.'

'Oh, Essaba,' said Awo again.

'Yes. That's my Mamaa alright. That's how she put it. Doesn't it make you sick to your stomach?'

'It does… it does,' Awo conceded mournfully.

Then one day, Esaaba and Paul had phoned home and spoken formally to her family. Several questions were asked and answered, some unease about origins was vaguely expressed but soon dispelled by instantly form-ulated wisdoms like:

'Oh, since they are both overseas,' *and therefore beyond our research capabilities and advice* and;

'Oh, since they are both overseas,' *and therefore our laws do not apply to them,* and;

'Oh, since they are both overseas,' *that should resolve any discrepancies in status and resulting complications.*

'In any case he is a white man.' Case closed!

In the end, the proper things had been done including bringing in some local mulattos to represent Paul's family. Everything culminated in a huge engagement party which most of the people who heard about it, either as guests or through hearsay, thought was the real wedding, but which turned out to be bigger than any real wedding they had ever been to. Mamaa could not have had it otherwise.

They say that Mamaa had danced so much at the party that people were scared she would pass out with sheer exhaustion. But, of course, Mamaa is strong and nothing like that had happened. The exhaustion showed the next morning though, when Mamaa confessed to being 'too tired to go to church.' She had never missed Sunday morning service. Ever. She always preferred the first service when she could make it. Otherwise, she would go for the second... No, Mamaa had not died that time from exertion. She had survived her daughter's engagement party. Only to store up her own surprise for her...

By some unspoken agreement from the earliest days of their friendship, the two young women never split the bill whenever they met and had anything to drink, or eat. One of them always settled it by turns, with them not bothering too much to remember who had paid the last time. So it is not strange that while Awo is looking for her purse Esaaba should have continued to sit staring into space. It is only after Awo leaves a tip inside the café folder, puts the rest of her change into her purse and looks at Esaaba to signal that they should be leaving, that she realises something is wrong. Esaaba has put her head on the table between her folded arms and she is weeping.

Awo shakes Esaaba on her shoulder, quite gently at first and then somewhat vigorously when she does not get any response. In fact, it seems as if the more she shakes Esaaba, the more rigid her friend's shoulder gets. The other surprise Awo registers is that with all the heaving, there are no tears to Esaaba's weeping. Then she stops shaking Essaba's shoulder and starts gently rubbing her back. After a while and thinking her friend is finally calm, she starts talking: first asking her what is wrong, then getting no answer back, reminding her that it is awfully late already and they should be leaving to go home. Nothing seems to get through to Esaaba. Until Awo murmurs something to the effect that whatever it is would be 'all right.' At that Esaaba sits straight up and gives a kind of whispered scream.

'No, it won't be all right,' she hisses at a rather startled Awo. 'Nothing is ever going to be all right,' she cries. 'Nothing, nothing, nothing…No, never.'

'What is it, Ess?'

'Nothing is ever going to be all right,' she cries out. 'Nothing, nothing, nothing,' she just keeps repeating. At this point Awo tells herself that she has to be calm. So in spite of the fact that she knows full well she should be getting home, she wiggles her backside more comfortably into the hard chair, takes her hands off her friend and folds them neatly on her lap, then she looks up and listens to Essaba rather calmly, as if neither of them has anywhere else to go. And Essaba is babbling on and especially catches Awo's attention when she says that someone has 'won out. She made me feel like a fool. Again. And forever.' The very simple question of who Esaaba is talking about is on the tip of Awo's tongue, but she pulls back from asking it because she's realised that Esaaba is talking about her mother.

'She had no right to do that to me. She had no right.'

'Ess, what did she do?'

'But I told you. I told you, didn't I?' Essaaba asks Awo with what is clearly a mixture of frustration and naked fury.

'Ess, what did you tell me?' Awo finds herself pleading.

'I told you that I had taken my children to show them off to her. And she should have sat up and taken a look at me and my children who are beautiful according to her own standards and more. That I had got my degree, had got a husband, a white man o, a white man and so she should sit up and look at us. Especially at the beautiful grandchildren I had produced for her...'

'Ow Ess...' Awo is thinking that this is much, much worse than anything she could have imagined.

'...But they met me at the airport, took me home, only to sit me down the moment we arrived and tell me that she was dead. Dead from a heart attack! Just to spite me? I should not have given her any notice of my visit. I should have just planned to surprise her. But no, with all my degrees, I could never be as clever as her. So of course, I warned her and she decided to up and die. Die! Rather than see a prosperous me and my children who are more handsome and prettier than she could ever have imagined.'

'Ow, Ess...' is all Awo can say. How can she ask her friend not to be ridiculous? She has heard of people dying from fear, from shock, from grief and even joy. But anyone dying from spite? Except that from all she is hearing, she can also imagine Esaaba's mother doing just that.

All this while, Awo and Esaaba have become something of a curiosity to the café staff and the other patrons who are sitting in their neighbourhood. But the two

58

friends are oblivious to all that. As the evening wears on, the place begins to empty.

Esaaba has not paused for even a second. But when she begins to pound the table, Awo gets truly alarmed. She realises that she cannot trust her friend on the Tube like this, or on a bus, or even in a taxi. She would have to go with her. And how can she? Their homes are on either side of Greater London and are great distances apart. And heaven knows she is already late… In fact she is certain that a couple of 'missed calls' on her phone must be from home…

So now, Awo has fished out her cell phone. She is calling Esaaba's husband Paul to come and take Esaaba home. Her next, and hopefully last, problem of the day is where to begin to tell Esaaba's story when her husband arrives at where she and her friend are sitting.

Recipe for a Stone Meal

Her mother hails from a matrilineal clan, her father from a patrilineage, at just over thirty-five years in the prime of life, 'reasonably good-looking,' 'strong' – her description of herself for herself – a qualified primary school teacher, married to another qualified school teacher and now public schools all over the country are back at work...

So what exactly is she doing here?

'Here' is a refugee camp. A refugee *what?* But the government says that this is the most peaceful country in the world... or at least in Africa.

Come again. Please. Because if you're joking, Sibi is not laughing. Not after watching her sister butchered by relatives on her mother's side and herself getting raped by men from her father's side, then four days of walking with two children to get here where she immediately had to stand for countless hours in the queue for this kilo of beans...

No news of James, her husband, yet...

The UN officers had told her to go and cook them, 'the way everyone is doing.' But she has boiled the beans all night and now that it's nearly noon, she has exhausted her ration of twigs and the kids have resumed their fretting from hunger. She has also exhausted her store of comforting words and gestures. And those beans are sitting in that new and shiny aluminum pot, harder to the touch now than when she first put them on the fire all those hours ago...

Look at her younger child passing out...

Someone is calling for a doctor...

He is examining the child. 'Oh, it's only from hunger,' he says, looking at the child with eyes that are clearly asking what kind of a mother would let her own child starve.

'It's those beans. They never got soft,' she wails.

'I know,' the doctor concedes. 'Actually, those beans were never meant to be cooked whole. Not under these circumstances anyway. They demand too much water, too much time and a lot of fire. Those UN characters should have brought only the powdered lot here. But maybe they could not be bothered. Or they sent the bags of powdered meal to their relatives at home.'

Then she too faints... just for some peace.

Notes

1. To the Memory of Honourable Hajia Hawa Yakubu.
2. "Recipe for a Stone Meal" was originally published in the inaugural issue of *Flash Magazine*, University of Chester – October 2008.

Feely-Feely

He had thought they understood one another. He had thought he had taken the trouble and the time to make sure of that; that as they were growing up, the boys would be clear about what to expect from him. That in some respects, he would go to any lengths on their behalf, while in others an inch would be too long.

Nothing had prepared him for this.

'I can't, you know,' Moses repeated for the ninth time that late afternoon.

'But why not?' Cobbie asked, his voice already higher than his father was used to.

'Because, because...,' Moses responded, childishly falling on an expression from as far back as primary school which everyone had used to annoy their class-mates whenever they didn't feel like answering questions or giving explanations. 'Cobbie, listen,' he began again, desperately, knowing that they weren't getting anywhere.

'Dad,' Cobbie called out, struggling to bring his voice down. 'My grades are extremely good. You see, it will not be a problem.' All said easily, but carefully too, as though

63

he was the father, and his father the unreasonable youngster who had to be coaxed to see sense.

'But that's my point,' Moses said, rather quickly, as though speed was of the essence.

'Your point?' questioned the son, wanting to laugh at his dear father and his ridiculous self. What was his point?

'Because you did quite well in the exams, I don't have to go and see anyone. If you had not done well, that would have been a problem. A different matter. This one is really straightforward. At least, that's my understanding. It should be quite simple.'

'Dad,' Cobbie said again, 'please listen to me. It is not straightforward, and it is not that simple.'

'Why not?' Moses pursued, almost foolishly.

'You see,' continued Cobbie, 'these days, whether you do brilliantly in the exams or fail outright, someone has to see somebody on your behalf…'

'Why?' The question escaped from Moses before he could swallow it.

'Because for every student who doesn't pass too well but is taken, some student who's done very well loses a place. Because as we all know, enrolment into our universities is severely limited.'

'But surely, not to people with good grades?' Moses persisted, surprised at himself.

'That doesn't make any difference anymore.' This time Cobbie screamed his lungs out.

'But excellent students like you…'

'Dad… Dad… D-a-d?!' Cobbie not only refused to

swallow the bait, but could not hide his complete and utter despair. He took a breath, and in the next instance seemed to have come to the conclusion that his father, who had never been as clever as other people's fathers, now seemed to have taken complete leave of what little sense he'd ever had. He, Cobbie, needed to be a little more patient with this new being.

'Dad,' Cobbie began again. 'If the system was open and depended only on grades, of course, there would be no problem. In fact, the choice for the universities is not necessarily between applicants who did well in the exams, and those who haven't done that well. Dad, we hear that these days, it's more often a question of who gets in from among so many BRILLIANT candidates.'

'Hmm…,' his father responded, not only calmly, but with a baffling absent-mindedness.

'Dad,' the younger man pressed on, 'even if I'd made A-plus grades in all my subjects, you would still have to go and see somebody at the University to secure my place.' He ended ferociously, and with an attempt at finality.

'Cobbie,' the father was pleading now. 'If I went to the campus and actually met with some people, I still wouldn't know what to say to them.'

'Why not?' the younger man asked, his voice at the point of breaking, but dangerous, like an old car on the brow of a hill, too tired to go forward, with its owner aware that going back was not an option.

'Because it's not in my nature to know what to say, or do, in such circumstances.'

'And what is your nature, Old Chap?' He had heard that when English boys wanted to put their fathers in their place, they would add 'old man,' 'old chap,' or some such appellation to their questions. But adding that one to that last question had been an accident. He had not meant to.

Moses winced. He began to plead openly. 'Please Cobbie, you know I'm an artist, a musician, a composer.'

Cobbie laughed. 'An artist! A musician!! A composer?!!' He looked at his father, and the look on his face was nakedly unbelieving. Inside he was thinking: so artists don't eat? Musicians don't shit? Composers' children have to lose out on life?

He couldn't stop laughing. His father in the meantime was thinking of all the crises they'd gone through since the boys were kids. Always over something he hadn't had, or didn't have, or something lacking in his personality, as compared to 'other people's fathers'. Now as Moses turned his back on the shards that were the relationship between him and his son, he looked through the nearest window. He could see that the western sky had turned red. More than ten shades of it. He found himself remembering what one of his uncles, a fisherman, had told him one day when he was a kid about how the evening skies always foretold the next day's catch...

Crises? They had gone through quite a few. The boys at nine and seven, declaring to him, that rather than driving them to and from school in his car, with all that smoke pouring out from the exhaust, he should ask the father of one of their friends to give them rides.

'Why?' he had asked them. 'Because everybody's father has a better car,' they had answered promptly, sounding very clear and convinced.

Then there had been, and remained, the matter of his clothes. For working in his study and being at home he wore *djellabahs* and *djebas*: long loose garments which were comfortable and sensible for this climate; a style much favoured by northern men of all types and classes, but clearly not considered appropriate modes of dressing for an educated, southern gentleman. Not that he wore them on formal occasions. Even then people, including his in-laws, had talked, and the children had heard them. He had not minded the talk, telling himself that he was not on this earth to dress to please other people. Until one day, as they were leaving the house to go and do some shopping, Cobbie had asked him why he didn't dress like other people's fathers? He had been so startled by the question that he'd actually tripped on the front doorsteps and nearly fallen. Then the boy had felt so bad, he had started to cry. He'd been seven then. Edum, his younger brother, joined in the wailing, so Moses decided to spare them whatever explanation he had, at least for the time being. About two weeks later, they had had one of those discussions. He had tried to explain why he preferred loose cotton garments, their appropriateness for the tropics and all that. The boys had seemed not to have heard him. And what they had heard they had clearly not understood.

…Then there was the day their mother had told Moses, right in front of the boys, that being well-known for his work as a musician was 'all fine, but not being able to afford a bicycle for your sons is really disgraceful.' 'Shame!' She had shouted. That was just before they discovered the illness. She died a year later. And Moses knew that he could only miss her on account of the boys who would grow up without her.

Cobbie was talking. 'Dad, I mean…other people's fathers are doctors, engineers, teachers, businessmen. You know, everybody knows what their work is. But you, who here knows what a composer is?' His voice was at once condemnatory and at the same time caressing, as though he was trying to soothe a colicky baby. 'Edum and I never had much pocket money. Not even half of what any of our friends seemed to have… Because you didn't seem to ever have much yourself. And now you are refusing to go and use your mouth to secure my place…Just your mouth, Dad.'

Cobbie had delivered this last speech first pacing the room, then moving towards the door into the courtyard, as if he'd meant to go out. There he'd stopped and stood, facing the door. There followed an incredibly long silence. Then, as if cued by a third person, they both turned and faced one another.

'Cobbie,' the father began, 'it will not just involve my mouth.'

'What do you mean?'

'It is also a question of principle.'

'Oh yes?'

'Yes.'

Cobbie turned to take hold of the doorknob.

'Listen...' said his father.

'I have listened, Dad.' Cobbie cut his father short, clearly and decisively, 'and I'm not going to continue listening to you... In fact, now you listen to me. If you can't go yourself to say something to anybody, then you should find some money, put it in an envelope, and give it to me. I'll do some research and find out the appropriate person to give it to, and how.'

'But... but I would be bribing somebody!' The father was truly shocked.

'Of course,' said Cobbie.

'But I can't.'

'Why not?'

'Because I think it's wrong and I never learned that art.'

'No? Well, Dad, the time has come for you to recognise a fact of life. That if bribery is wrong, people still do it and you too must learn to bribe... Yes, my goodie-goodie father, it's time you learnt "that art"!' Cobbie had clearly decided to abandon patience and caution. 'In any case, did you hear me a second ago when I suggested that you just find the money, put it into an envelope and I'll find a way to do the rest?'

'I can't,' Moses declared miserably.

'If you loved me, you would try,' Cobbie challenged, deliberately.

Moses collapsed. He did not fall down. He just shrank instantly, like a deflated balloon. He sat down, and put his head in his hands. But Cobbie had not finished with him. 'It's being rumoured that the universities' registries are coming out with full lists of enrolments in two weeks. Please, go and see somebody this week. Otherwise my name will not appear on any of them.' He finished with unmistakable finality, opened the door, shut it carefully and softly, with a reverence normally reserved for the very ill, or the recently dead, then he went out.

They say that the next two weeks were pure and simple hell for father and son. They never spoke to one another. Cobbie went on believing that his father 'would do something.' And initially, so did Moses. But in the end, he couldn't bring himself to go to the campus, or put money in an envelope for Cobbie. Then one morning, the dailies came out with the National Lists of Enrolment into State-Accredited Universities (the acronym NALESAU, was wickedly nicknamed THESAW). Cobbie went through the list for his first choice university. His name was nowhere. Then he went through the lists for his second and third choices. Ditto. He went over all three again. Same result. After the sixth and most thorough scrutiny, he gave up. He had told himself that he was most probably too stressed out to spot his name among all the others. Perhaps there had been a mess up in the lists' alphabetical order, as nearly always happened. So he turned the entire project over to Edum. His brother spent the rest of the day on the job. He even went through the lists of the other universities his brother had not bothered to apply to. But nothing came out of all the effort. By the time they decided to give up on the enterprise completely, it was dark. Cobbie had not eaten the whole day. Later he couldn't remember whether he had even drunk anything. He went to bed anyway.

The next day, Cobbie woke at dawn. He folded all the newspapers neatly and went to stand before his father's bedroom door where Moses was sleeping with their stepmother. He knocked, and when he heard 'come in' he opened it, entered the room and without greeting them, dumped the newspapers on the floor by his father's side of the bed. Then he walked out again, shutting the door behind him. If he heard his father calling his name, he didn't acknowledge it with even a second's pause in his stride.

He just walked on and on?

That's what I heard... They say he hadn't spoken to his younger brother either. He kept walking out of the house and into town. And that was the last time anyone saw or heard of him in this country.

In twenty years?

In twenty-eight-and-a-half years to be exact.

And what happened to his father?

They say when he got out of bed that fateful morning, he went straight to the cupboard where he kept his drinks, took a big gulp of some alcohol and could never stop drinking after that... Now we know that Cobbie left the country soon after and went overseas. In his new country, he continued his education, became a doctor, married a daughter of

71

*that land, had children, then he became a citizen of
that country and even enlisted in the army...*

*Do you mean that he had gone to fight for his new
country?*

*And why not? Actually he had not had to fight...
But he was certainly at some war front or other,
as an army medic.*

*And now he is coming back here as that country's
ambassador?*

You heard right.

Someone whistled sharply.

Yes, yes.

How is that possible?

*Why shouldn't that be possible? What century do you
think we are living in?*

The twenty-first.

*Okay, then please, organise the space around you,
put your bag firmly under your seat, and fasten your
seat belt...*

Did anyone whistle sharply again, anywhere around?

....

Note: "Feely-Feely" was first published in: *Wasafiri*, Volume 19, Issue 42,
Summer 2004, pages 34–36.

Rain

She had asked him whether they were walking through a Christmas tree plantation.

'Forest,' he had corrected her affectionately, with that maddening twinkle in his eyes, half a smile around his mouth and trying very hard not to make her feel ignorant.

He had guessed early on that communication between them was not going to be easy. But he had not known how very hard. Everything came to them loaded with implications. Everything. The sun, the moon, clothes, music and all other art forms. Food and drink? Definitely. And not just the regular jokes about black coffee, *café au lait* and chocolate. But crazier references to chicken... you know... dark meat, light meat... And there were all those sinister stories that had been read to him when he was a baby, as well as those he had discovered for himself when he began to find books to read at home and in school. Horrible references that he is now convinced had been deliberately sneaked into lovely stories to ruin them for him. Just look at what they did with silly old Tintin. Tales about white missionaries and

73

black pots and such... Stories that used to fill his sleep with nightmares which he had forgotten, or thought he had forgotten but clearly had not, because soon after they met, they came up like messengers from home, from his mother to be specific, to remind him what he'd been told and taught about Africa and Africans. And they stayed with him, the messengers did, not showing any signs that they would want to go back anytime soon to where they'd come from, if ever, and also refusing to be sent away. Which was worse.

'A Christmas tree plantation' is how she had described the forest. She was precious. And that's what they were, no? Or what she had met them as. It really was true that she had first encountered fir trees on Christmas cards with Santa Claus and his sleigh and reindeer – with plenty of snow and sometimes a very green plant with red berries which one English art teacher had shown them how to draw. The teacher had told the class that this other plant was called holly. In those days, everything about Christmas was also religious. So they had thought that related places like Nazareth and Bethlehem were all in heaven. Therefore it was with some disappointment that they came to learn later that these locations are actually here on earth, though still somewhat far away: the River Jordan, Jerusalem, Egypt. She had thought as a child that you would have to die before getting to these places and seeing them for real.

And the teacher. Wasn't she supposed to be Irish or Scottish and not English? Hmm... much of the time, we were not aware of those differences and when we were, they did not seem to matter much about how they related to us, or how we were expected to relate to them. No, not very much.

Very much intrigued, but still sounding doubtful, he had chuckled, 'Is it true?'

'Yes,' she had replied again, some slight irritation showing. Then sensing a need to explain herself just a little more, she had added: 'I mean... that was when I was a kid. Of course, later, I knew from geography and maybe even religious studies that those are real places where people still live.' What she did not add was that even as a young adult and a secondary school student, her imagination had still had a problem with snow and Santa Claus and his sleigh and reindeer, as well as Christmas trees which she is now learning are called fir trees and the very green plant with the red berries that the art teacher had told them was called holly...

Matty was repeating in his head: 'Cute but incorrect. Like so many of the ideas she has about my background.' Then he caught his breath. 'Cute but incorrect?' He couldn't say the same about many of the ideas he had had about her background. Nothing about those could be described as 'cute.' Scary and not too correct would be more like it. He had shivered ever so slightly and she had picked up on that immediately. 'Are you okay?' she'd wondered aloud. He had nodded, his lips narrowing even more with the puzzlement of everything. That's the other thing about the people here she was finding impossible to understand. By her standards, it was cold – a full six months of the year and possibly more. She would say very cold in fact. Yet she'd noticed that as soon as the height of summer was over, they began to shiver at the slightest drop in temperature. When she asked him why people acted as though they too were new to the cold, he'd answered quite simply that no one ever gets used to it. It was nearly eight o'clock in the evening, but it looked very much earlier since it was the middle of summer and still light enough for him to see all the features on her face clearly.

She'd been in the country for about two years to continue studying French and had another two or so years to go. Halfway through that second year, she and Matty had met at a reception following a lecture that some visiting African dignitary had delivered at one of the town's main libraries. She had observed that the hall was mostly packed with older women and some elderly men. In that crowd of nearly two hundred people, there had been only a handful of people she had considered young like her. So she kept wondering about who those older people were and why they were there. She knew why she was there alright.

Affiye lived with Appau, an older relative and a paternal uncle who had left home in his youth to come to Europe, had lived here all his life and who, unlike other people's relatives, had never returned home even for visits. This was the uncle whom as a kid she had heard spoken of in whispers, as though he was some sort of a mysterious being, until out of nowhere he had got in touch and much to the utter amazement of everybody, proceeded to send money home regularly to pay the school fees for a number of the younger members of the family, including her. So it was her 'Uncle Appau' who, after encouraging her to 'take French seriously' in secondary school, had brought her over to go to university and continue with her study of the language. Appau was by then in his sixties and as far as Affiye could figure out, he and his wife, a woman of that country, were both very old. Affiye knew that for a very long time before she joined them her uncle Appau and his wife Gretchen had lived alone. Their two sons were busy with their own lives in some other cities and only came home at Christmas with their families: a wife and a daughter for one; and a wife, two sons and a daughter for the other.

The first time Appau had asked her to go to a meeting with him she'd complied out of curiosity. But then, much to her surprise, she had subsequently enjoyed herself very much listening to the lecture and mingling during the cocktails. The visitor's presentation had been interesting and the discussion period that followed had been lively. However, what had also attracted her attention had been the interaction between her uncle Appau and his friends on the one hand and the visitor on the other. After attending a couple more meetings with her uncle, Affiye was curious to realise that he was one of a group of African men in town who never missed a public present-ation by visiting African writers and scholars, government officials and other experts. They would sit there listening to the speakers with rapt attention and then ask awkward questions and make crazy remarks during the discussion period following a presentation. This, she concluded much later, was calculated to impress the white people in the audience, while all the while they were updating themselves on matters at home.

The topic on that first occasion was the dynamics of the divestiture of state enterprises, or something like that. Later, Affiye couldn't remember whether the visiting expert had been in favour of that particular government policy or not. What he had tried to do, as dispassionately as possible, was to show how terribly divestiture had been handled so far, because of the 'you-scratch-my-back-I-scratch-yours' attitude that had prevailed, and which allowed the big people of every government and its opposition to loot the state through under-invoicing, over-invoicing and other criminal means. Did he have any solutions? Yes. He and other economists with similar views had been trying for years to get a hearing. But much of the time no one would listen to them. And when they were listened to, no one thought their ideas should be acted upon. Clearly, the speaker knew what he was talking about.

However, it seemed to Affiye that no matter how hard he tried, the speaker could not shake off the attacks. In the framing of their questions and other comments, her uncle and his friends struggled to get the rest of the audience to think that they were the experts and the visitor was only an ignorant, elitist bully. Elitist he probably was – at home anyway. But ignorant? Meanwhile, they succeeded in humbling the speaker. After all, consciously worked out or not, they had had time to perfect their strategy, while the hapless speaker was clearly caught off his guard.

The first time Affiye realised what her uncle Appau and his friends were doing, she was surprised, then bewildered and then ashamed. When the pattern kept repeating itself with every meeting they attended together, she became outraged. So although she continued to go with him, it was from a mixture of duty and boredom. At one point, she'd tried to confront her uncle about their attitude. But he shouted at her and told her flatly that he did not know what she was talking about. When she persisted, he said something to the effect that if those visiting experts knew so much, why was the situation at home still so bad?

Affiye had had no answer for Appau, but her feelings of unease had not disappeared either. She became more and more reluctant to attend the meetings with her uncle but without summoning the necessary courage to refuse. After all, she was all of twenty-three or thereabouts, while Appau was in his sixties. Not to mention the fact that he was the one who had put her through school, paid the bill for the trip to Europe, paid for her passport and visa, paid for the air ticket and for the clothes on her back. And now it was this same 'Uncle Appau' who was footing the bill for everything to do with her being here in this country: room, board, clothes, university tuition, plus some pocket money to boot. No, nothing in her upbringing had prepared her to say 'no' to someone like her uncle on any issue, at anytime or in any place. There was only one day when she really could not make it to a meeting with him. And that was because she had some kind of a raging fever and Appau himself had nearly not gone because of that. But it was that once only.

Affiye's mother was known to remark that 'life has a wild womb,' whenever she felt irritated by the way life has a way of every now and then throwing something quite ridiculous and unpleasant our way. Or even delighting us with a glorious gift out of the blue. Affiye was to learn that actually, her mother had edited the original proverb, which was of course nothing if not profane or crude or both. Rather odd in a society that frowned on any public mention of human sexual parts. As a good Muslim woman, Affiye's mother could never have allowed herself to be heard using such words. Not even to herself.

Affiye's mind must have filed her mother's version of the proverb for when she was old enough to remember to use it. This was years later. But there she was, remembering it one day in a land faraway from where both she and the proverb were born. Because if life doesn't have a rather wild womb, how could it be, that on a day that Affiye was most reluctant to go to a meeting with Appau but she had gone anyway because she could not refuse to go and was inwardly swearing that that was to be the absolute last time come what may – that was also the day and the occasion when she met Matty?

It was during refreshments. The small number of young people in the audience had found themselves in a group. So here they were with their fruit juices and sodas, teas and coffees, cakes, cheeses and other assorted finger foods. They were arguing good-naturedly about issues from the presentation and its follow-up discussion. When someone said hello from close by, Affiye said hello back, before raising her head to look into a pair of grey eyes that were somewhat higher above her own. They smiled at each other.

'I am Mathias Koessler,' he said.

'Hi,' was all Affiye said back.

Both of them became aware that she had not supplied her name. He did not insist. Later, neither could remember if they had spent any time talking and if so what about. But on the way back home, each of them wished they had exchanged phone numbers. So there was some solid regret there. In the interim, Affiye had forgotten she had sworn that this was the last event she would attend with her uncle. Rather, here she was wishing for one more such opportunity to come along. It did. And for the occasion, Affiye took a little more trouble with how she looked before she and her uncle set out. If Appau noticed any difference in her mood he didn't comment.

Mathias too had been ready. As soon as he learnt of the public lecture he knew that she would be there. So of course they bumped into one another. The hall was not quite full when Mathias made a beeline for an empty seat next to Affiye. He said 'hello' and sat down with a 'may I?' in his eyes, which had not appeared on his lips. During refreshments, they moved away to be with the other students and then into a twosome at the edge of that group.

'Now please, what's your name?' Mathias asked.

'Affiye,' Affiye replied. There followed a second's silence.
'So you came again?' each of them said.
'Yes,' they both replied.
'Why?' they asked in unison again. At that they burst out laughing and quite loudly, so that a few people nearby turned to look at them. That's when they quickly exchanged phone numbers and split up.

There followed an eternity when sometimes Appau either did not go to the talks, or went but did not ask Affiye to come along. She kept wondering why she did not have the courage to ask her uncle about it and certainly did not have the courage to go alone. Years later, she was to scold herself for all that, because with hindsight, she could see no reason why she stayed away. With a lot of regret, she reminded herself that most of those events had been in the late afternoon anyway. She could easily have gone to the meetings instead of the library for instance and got home early enough for her uncle and his wife not to worry about her whereabouts. And if she had gone and she and Appau had bumped into one another, she would not have been the one to have had to do any explaining. That task would clearly have fallen on her uncle. Of course, none of that had occurred to her then. Where she came from, it was always expected of the youth that they try to figure out what the older generation was thinking and planning and then get themselves blamed for any erroneous thought-reading. Indeed and normally, younger persons were expected to apologise, even when they were the wronged party! Affiye became aware of all that only later and then admitted how much, in her zeal to be a 'good girl,' she had allowed her society to cramp her style and ultimately to hurt her. But all that was later. Much, much, later…

At one point, Mathias Koessler had concluded that Affiye was staying away to avoid him, but still he went to nearly every single public lecture where the speaker was African. He also began to call the number Affiye had given him. He phoned a couple of times, but was informed on each occasion that Affiye was not in. It was usually her uncle's wife who answered the phone and reported it to her, since she was in more often than the other two. When Appau answered it, he didn't bother to say anything to Affiye.

In the end, Affiye called Matty from a public phone booth to tell him that she'd rather he didn't phone her again. It turned out to be the longest phone conversation they were ever going to have. At first, she wouldn't tell him why she thought they should not see one another again. And because Matty sensed that if he let Affiye put down the receiver it would be the last time they would be in touch, he concentrated on just getting her to promise to phone him again. When she finally agreed to that, he was so relieved he almost wept. Then he was even more relieved that she wasn't there to see him. He pulled himself together quickly and in the voice of a rather smart negotiator, asked her to specify a time and a place for them to meet. After some hesitation, she gave in to that too and they agreed to meet at one of the cafés on campus. From then on they met regularly: at cafés, in the library, or sometimes at the cinema where they would watch matinee films together. In the end she relaxed completely in his company.

'Matty, you see how different the two of you are?'
His mother's messengers arrive promptly and in full
force. 'I think that it would be better if she were a
little less dark: maybe like an Arab… or an Indian
or a Latina. But a real black African? Matty, that's
too much. Rather gross. No?'

At such moments, it was always quite hard for Matty to figure out whether the grossness referred to Affiye's skin colour only, or *'la situation entire,'* as he suspected his mother would have described their relationship. Meanwhile and as usual, the messengers were being their persistent selves.

'I think she will not be good for you. So much
blackness?! My Lord. If you don't believe me, why
don't the two of you try standing in front of the
mirror together?'

His heart would lurch rather badly so that it took some considerable energy and concentration for him not to scream aloud. But he managed. After all, the last thing he wanted was to have Affiye think he was crazy. So although the messengers kept hanging around, he refused to respond to the vicious innuendos. Besides, like the sign of the cross to a ghoul, his happiness kept the tightness of uncertainty from squeezing out his heart completely.

The coordinator of the retreat on the 'Impact of Gold Mining in Africa on Local Populations' must have been excellent at her job, because the flyers announcing it were all over the campus. Not only were interested individuals asked to register but it seemed as if that's not all they were expected to do. Following registration, they would be contacted. Planned to last from Sunday evening to Saturday morning, it sounded as if everything would be free: accommodation, meals and snacks. The only aspect of the programme that was somewhat restricted was the number of participants. Fifty individuals would be selected from those who registered early.

If anyone had thought there was anything odd about such an event taking place somewhere in Europe instead of somewhere in Africa, they didn't say so any time before, during or after the retreat. In any case, if they had, they would only have exposed their own ignorance. For over a century, all sorts of meetings, conferences and other caucuses crucial to Africa and her peoples had been organised outside that continent and most especially in Europe. Affiye and Matty had seen the notices independently and each of them had decided to register and then persuade the other to register, so that both of them would end up at the retreat. The plan worked.

The five or so days had been full of intense discussions. From the beginning, it had been obvious that the organisers had not wanted any minute unplanned. Each day began with the obligatory plenary and the presentation of research papers. This was followed by group sessions programmed around specific issues, which in turn were followed by the evening plenary. Then there were mealtimes and morning and afternoon coffee breaks. Very clearly, the idea behind the retreat was not to afford people any time to contemplate the state of their souls. However, Matty and Affiye still found time to explore the area a lot more thoroughly than they had been able to do during the entire semester. They found themselves doing that every night of the retreat, without any prior discussion or planning.

Now here they were crossing the road, going over the small bridge and then turning to the left of the stream and sitting on the embankment though not before each of them had first taken off their sandals. Mathias rolled up his jeans. Affiye was in a short skirt and therefore all right anyway. They sat with their feet dangling in the cool waters of the stream. Then they began playing with the water, spraying it up and down and sideways, their feet sometimes touching. They always did this the moment they got to the stream and sat down. Some days that's all they did. They played until both of them were completely exhausted and then got up and walked away. On other days, they would do their foot splashing, then get up and walk around for some time before returning to the camp. At such times, they hardly talked. But it was unclear why not. Maybe it was one of those relationships for which words are not needed at all. And then there was this awkward business of communicating in a language that belonged to neither of them. In spite of a living and working relationship with English all her life, Affiye had come to believe those who described her as only a Speaker-of-English-as-a-Second-Language.

Meanwhile Matty had told her once that as a young boy, he had learned to speak and write English because it was 'cool to.' After all, English was not only the language across the Channel, but also of the United States of America.' Now he knows, as a post-doctoral research scientist in microbiology, that it was a smart gift he had given himself. 'Oh, but it is wonderful!' he had once exclaimed.

'What is?' Affiye had asked, genuinely puzzled.

'English,' he'd replied. 'English... English...' He was virtually singing.

'Well, what about it?'

And then he couldn't explain himself. How could he tell her that he couldn't possibly have talked to her at all in his own language since every word, every syllable acquired a totally unsavoury meaning when uttered in her presence? English then was something of a safety valve. Of course, as a European language, he was sure English was as bad as his on the whole blackness business. In fact he'd come to suspect that it was worse. But he kept telling himself that the burden it brought him was lighter. That he didn't own English. It was not his mother tongue. Therefore he could not be held responsible for any of its craziness.

When they talked, or rather, when she talked, it was mostly about the river. How beautiful and cool it was. Quite often, she would just talk about water generally, praising its life-giving, life-saving properties. Or in some other ecstatic way that he found a little unsettling as though she had just come from a place where water was not known. In the beginning, he would listen, absolutely enthralled and relishing the way she was making him look at water in a way that he had never done before. But then after a while he began to feel a little uneasy and even apprehensive, at what seemed to be some kind of obsession of hers. So once in a while, he would try and think of something to say that was not quite a criticism of her, but which he hoped would put a little damper on her enthusiasm. Like reminding her of how voracious and dangerous water can be. 'People drown, you know,' he said, with a vehemence that was quite out of character.

Sailors at work.
Voyagers on business and at play.
Fishermen at sea. Anglers on land.
We drown in rivers and lakes and ponds.
Swimming pools and bathtubs.
Rain storms that kill…

She never seemed to listen to him and when she did, never seemed to have heard him. She would ramble on and on about how little water they had at home. As a child, she knew the distances her mother's people and later her mother had had to walk with their plastic containers looking for water. And when they got the water it was in a sorry state, which at the time she was not even aware of.

*The colour alone was enough to petrify and drinking
could kill and often killed. Sundry bugs and germs,
toads' eggs and frog excrement, pretty dragonflies
skating and dropping wings, dead leaves from gusty
winds...*

It didn't help her to remember that from all she'd read
and heard, her mother's place wasn't the worst off on her
continent. That in Africa there were places where water
was so scarce, occasionally people had to drink their own
urine to stay alive and died when their bodies didn't have
enough water to produce urine.

*Ei Africa.
By the way, is it really true about water and
Ethiopia?
What about water and Ethiopia?
Haven't you heard?
What haven't I heard?
The Nile above?
That I know.
The water below?
What water below?
Listen, the rumour is that Ethiopia sits on an
aquifer so huge it might be the largest in the world.
That put to all sorts of uses, that country cannot
only feed itself, but half of Africa and all of Western
Europe too...
What?
Yes.*

Maybe it's just that. A rumour.
Oh, Africa.

'Mathias, you have so much water here. So much,' she exclaimed, apropos of nothing, Mathias was to recall later with some confusion.

'Yes? As compared to where?' he asked warily.

As far as he could remember from school trips and family holidays to the other lands in Europe, they had as much water as his country. You got up in the morning, went to pee into the toilet bowl, flushed it, brushed your teeth, washed your face or even had a full shower, then ate some breakfast of one kind or another... Of course you did all that with water. And you took it all for granted. Just like the water you used at home. Come to think of it, since he'd never been anywhere beyond his continent, what could he possibly know about the rest of the world and water?

'Really, what kind of life would it be if one was aware of every cup of water one used in the course of a whole day?' This is the type of question he congratulated himself for daring to ask aloud.

'Actually, that's how it is where I come from,' she pursued. 'But you have all these rivers... Like this one...'

Mathias was beginning to feel accused, as though he personally owned all the rivers of Europe. 'But this is not a river. It is just a small stream.'

'As far as I am concerned, it is a river.' She said this with finality and moved her head off his shoulder. He noticed the gesture. 'It is bigger than any river that we have at home. And I am sure it doesn't disappear in the dry season…'

'This is bigger than any river in the whole of your country?' he asked with some alarm.

'Oh no,' she responded rather quickly, too quickly, somewhat ashamed for alarming him, for the unnecessary exaggeration. 'No. I was only referring to my mother's part of the country.'

> *The NGOs do it all the time. Home-grown or foreign-based. How else were we going to effectively pull at those liberal heart-strings unless we exaggerated Africa's woes just a wee bit?*

She got up, turned left and crossed the bridge, as though she was going to run 'home' that very minute. So he too stood up, turned left and trotted after her as if to stop her. When she sensed him close-by, she wheeled around and screamed, 'You people don't even ever get a dry season.' That came out as both a realisation and an accusation.

'Maybe not,' he replied quietly, but without conviction. Even this small opinion he had expressed rested on the fact that he really did not know what a dry season meant. There will be no water coming through the pipes or what?

'You see?!' she said triumphantly, 'I am right. You don't even have a dry season.'

Now he accepted that he stood completely accused.

'Season… season…,' he began, 'there is spring and summer…'

'Y-e-s...'

'...there is autumn.'

'Y-e-s...'

'...then there is winter... Affi, there are four seasons...'

'And no room for a fifth.'

'Well, well...'

'Well what?'

'And in the winter, there is snow. Plenty of it... then the snow melts and becomes water, water... Plenty of water... Oh, Affi,' he said.

'I know you don't understand,' she declared mournfully, with no hint of irony. It had sounded more like 'I know you cannot understand.' She moved closer to lean on his shoulder.

'But I do,' he had replied too quickly, unconvincingly again. In the moments that followed, he was quiet while asking himself how else to respond to her. Certainly not by telling her the truth: that he not only did not understand her, but he was becoming quite nervous about where all her anxiety about water was leading them.

Back sitting on the embankment, they went into their normal cozy silence. Or they tried to. What then was new that day was this. Unlike all the other times when their feet touched and they just carried on playing, this time they sat as though stung and they both stopped throwing water about. There they sat, still for a very long time, each of them apparently lost in his and her thoughts. She began to cry in a heartrending low sob that was followed by more soft sobs. Then the weeping gained momentum and rose into a proper wail.

Mathias moved to pull her nearer to him. She pushed him away. After that he didn't know what else to say or do. So he did nothing and said nothing. He just sat as if glued to his spot on the embankment, while she continued to weep enough tears to rival the waters of the stream. But she had to stop at some point. And when she did, they both got up and quietly walked back to the conference centre.

They had not planned their departure from the conference centre or how they were going to go to their separate abodes. Maybe parting hadn't been on their minds. The following morning, they sat together at one of the long breakfast tables, as they had done the previous day. But instead of the usual lively chat between the two, or some kind of a discussion with the other people, each of them just sat in silence. Somehow, they had not found it possible to speak to one another again.

And then it was time to leave. Later, in different worlds and at different times, each of them often revisited the time between that last visit to the river and that morning at breakfast; the retreat breaking up; people getting on different buses depending on where in town they were headed for. And then that fleeting moment when they had each caught the other looking and they had not said a word to one another. They were to wonder separately and endlessly, what could have got into them. The heartbreak that was always like a slow burning fire in her would occasionally flare up and attack her guts, so that she would have to find somewhere very quickly to throw up. And it would leave her sweating and completely drained of energy. As for him, it was a headache: that heartbreak. Much of the time, it was like a low-grade but rather persistent migraine which would explode on occasion into some absolutely and unimaginably violent pain. Although these attacks were mercifully short, they also left him sweating profusely and drained of all energy. Later still, each of them would experience dizzy spells, whose causes were a mystery to different doctors on both sides of the Atlantic.

At the beginning of her third year in the country, Affiye and her uncle found themselves amicably discussing her future and agreeing that she would go home once she had graduated, work for a year or so and then return to Europe to do some postgraduate study. Every now and then during the year, Affiye had thought of asking Appau whether they could shift the plan around a bit to let her stay a little longer studying or working, or both. However, she never seemed to feel strongly enough about that line of action to pursue it with Appau.

She had not taken any phone calls from Matty since the retreat, so there was no way he could have known that she was leaving. And now here she was about two weeks from departure, with all her bags packed or nearly and having to admit that she did not want to leave. At all. The remaining days were consumed with last minute shopping, air ticket confirmation and other such preparations. Then she was on the plane on her way back home.

Just before she left and as part of the preparations for her departure, her uncle had had a discussion with her about her immediate future. On his side the conversation was often heavy with foreboding, clearly based on some of the issues that had kept him away from his native country for so long and might prevent him from ever even visiting. If it all sounded pathetic, Affiye was not about to say so.

'Affiye,' he began gently one day. 'Have you thought of where you'll go and stay when you arrive?' The question had taken her by surprise.

'No,' she confessed.

'Well,' Appau continued, 'no matter what time you get off the plane, given that all our Accra homes are quite a distance from the airport and nearly all our relatives are poor workers and others who are trying to just get by in the informal sector, it will not be a good idea to plan to go home straightaway.'

And Affiye was thinking, 'but this man has not been back in our country for nearly thirty years. So how can he know all this?'

'In fact, their living conditions must be quite hard if all the stories we hear are true...'

'And here he is answering a question I hadn't even asked, as though he can read my mind!'

'...I know our people. Even if you won't mind sharing their modest homes, none of them will feel confident to ask you to stay with them.'

'Yes. I mean no.'

'So what shall we do?'

That was when she remembered Aba Sarah, an old school friend, whose parents were well-off enough to have a house with guest quarters. She had phoned and discussed her predicament. Sarah had given her her parents' number which she had passed on to her uncle. Soon enough, 'we've worked something out' was how Appau had put the arrangement he had made with the parents of Affiye's friend. And that's how Aba Sarah and her people came to be at the airport the evening Affiye flew back in. She was met by a team of relatives comprising eleven individuals. Her mother and three other adult relatives had come all the way from the north. The rest were made up of extended family members in town, including two giggly girls who looked like they were still in their teens. From the airport, they had separated. Affiye had left with her friend and her parents. Her mother and the others had gone to stay with relatives in the city.

Affiye had woken up quite early the next morning. So that by the time Sarah came to call her for breakfast, she was ready to leave. But neither Sarah nor her parents were quite prepared for Affiye's plans for the rest of the day, which she promptly announced the moment they all sat down to breakfast. Sarah's parents tried to explain to Affiye about the reality of jet lag and the need for her to take things slowly for the next few days. She listened intently while nodding her head politely. When she was sure they had said their bit, she tried to explain her side of the story. That in the short time they had had time to talk before they all parted, her mother and the relatives had made it clear to her that they felt quite hurt she had not wanted to go home with them. 'As if we don't have a room in this whole town fit for our daughter to sleep in,' was the pained chorus from her cousins and aunts. But she had begged them to let her follow the previous arrangement, on condition that she would meet them in the morning and later move in with those relatives whose home was not too far from Sarah's parents.

'Plus,' and she said this with utmost respect, 'I don't want to come across to my relatives as one of those over-civilised know-all smart alecks.' Even Sarah's parents had to laugh at that. They admitted that Affiye had a point and a compromise was duly struck. She would go and meet her mother and other relatives that morning but would return to stay with them for a couple of days more. So she had her day's outing, but returned to the Airport Residential Area. Over the next three or four days she virtually did nothing but eat and sleep. From then on, Aba Sarah's home became her home. Even after she found a job and settled into her own apartment, it remained her principal family home in the city and the parents expected her to drop by whenever she could, until Aba Sarah began to accuse Affiye of stealing her boyfriends and things got rather awkward between the two friends. But that, as they say, is another very long story.

The first time Affiye visited her father's family house in Accra, her cousin Minnie lamented knowingly that she should have got herself a white husband because 'white men know how to take care of a woman. Not like these beasts here.' Affiye had cringed. 'As for these men, you slave to look after them and for thanks, they beat you. Day in, day out.' Affiye would have cringed some more but for remembering with some amusement that for her cousin Minnie (whom everyone referred to as 'Auntie' anyway), 'day in day out' was a phrase she applied to every unpleasantness. In fact, behind her back, Affiye and the rest of the younger relatives called Minnie 'Day-In-Day-Out.' Affiye eventually learned that Minnie had just returned home from life as a high-end prostitute in Abidjan, and was gloriously rich.

Affiye regretted that the male African students at her university had treated her like she was carrying the plague because she was dating a white boy, never mind that they dated white girls with the zeal of religious devotees…

Later in Tamale, when Lamisi came to see her, it was like the past eleven or so years had not happened. He was the youngest of her maternal uncles and younger than Affiye. And since she had been an only child for a very long time, the two of them had bonded in a rather sibling sort of way. And now meeting again, they had immediately started trading confidences like they used to. But, she was to wish that following these shared confidences, her dear Lamisi would not have periodically asked about her 'Visigoth' while crinkling up his nose…

Much to her surprise, it had taken Affiye some time to get a job in Accra. She was not sure where she'd got the idea from, but she had had it. That in her generation's slang, she'd 'land a cool job' as soon as she started looking for one. She was to learn better.

'By the way, did you know that in these parts, employers do not always bother to send rejection letters?'

'What do you mean?'

'Like they advertise the jobs all right, call people for interviews, then *tsim*! The trail freezes.'

'W-h-a-a-t!'

'Please don't "what" me. Sometimes they might even invite you for interview number two if you are lucky to be on the short list. Then flam and komm, it's dead silence in the city.'

'But why?'

'Please don't ask me why. Can be anything. The job was always going to go to a close friend or an extended relative: a niece, a nephew. Or to the friend's son or daughter. In recognition of the ties that bind, or as a reciprocal favour for other favours received, or anticipated…'

In the end, Affiye was lucky. After a whole bewildering year of applications and rejections stated and unstated, she did land a job. And quite a cool one too. Her background in French had come in handy. She found a job assisting a powerful management consultant firm in the city as the Liaison Officer for International Affairs. Which of course was a grand way to describe the company's relationship with Ghana's three Francophone neighbours. Affiye discovered that although her boss was quite driven, she was not the growling leopard people spoke of. They worked together for three years. Then the boss fell in love, got married and merged her name and her business with her new husband's. Like the other three 'senior officers,'

Affiye's job disappeared in the merger. She was laid off. But rather grandly. With those three years' experience under her belt and a glowing recommendation in her hand, she discovered the joy of knowing that this time around, she could not only get a job quite easily, but could even have chosen from a handful.

She had been back home for four years, during which time she had avoided any form of communication with Matty, despite the fact that he was always on her mind. Always. And so much that she talked endlessly to everybody about him. Yet she refused to answer his letters and postcards, refused to answer his emails, refused to give him her phone number and when he dug that number out somehow, she hung up on him when he called.

No, marriage had not been on her mind. She seemed to have been too busy for such matters. And in any case, how could she contemplate dating anybody else with Matty occupying her thoughts, her dreams and her nightmares? And no, she had lost all appetite for returning to Europe. She let her job eat up all the usable hours of the working week, and then some. Once in a while, she would go home to the village in the North to see her mother. Meanwhile though, most of her weekends were taken up with family and extended family matters.

The other discussion her uncle Appau had had with her just before she left Europe was in connection with the education of their younger relatives, now that she was going to be home. So she found herself at the great age of twenty-nine parenting at least a dozen youngsters through schools in the north and the south of the country. In fact, for those in the southern sector, she was not just paying their school fees and the endless levies, buying regular uniforms and the annual Independence Day parade wear. She also found herself checking on grades, talking to teachers and school heads and of course attending PTA meetings whenever possible.

If Affiye sometimes wondered how her life could already be so cluttered, she did not discuss it with anybody. There was no one to discuss it with. Or so she had felt. Every now and then she had thought of bringing it up with her mother. But she had held back since two of the youngsters were her mother's children anyway: a boy and a girl who were the last of the four her mother had finally had after all those years of anxiety that Affiye would be her last.

'Affiye, are you a witch that your mother can't have any more children? Don't you want a brother? Or a sister? Do you want to be an only child forever?' And her eyes would well up with unshed tears since she wanted brothers and sisters very much, in fact, very, very much. She who was almost always the only one in her class who didn't have brothers and sisters and had had no idea what to do to help her mother to improve the situation...

Then, God being so kind, the problem righted itself, or got righted somehow. When Affiye's mother divorced her father and returned to her home in the North, she remarried and began to have children again, when Affiye was already fifteen years old. And now, here they were, spilling on to the adult Affiye as ready-made responsibilities and sources of major preoccupation.

Her life was not without other more private and personal problems though. The biggest of them, she would tell herself ruefully, was of her own making. She had quite regularly met young men who had more than a passing interest in her. But she was often unmoved by them. And even when she began dating them, she found herself freezing up. Then there were those non-starter occasions, when she had met young men her friend Aba Sarah had been dating, only for them to turn their attention to her. And with some rather embarrassing persistence, in spite of her very spirited rejection of them. She never thought for a moment during those years of marriage.

But today, Affiye is getting married.

'Affiye is getting married?'

'Yes.'

'Thank you, Our Father God.'

'Is it true that Affiye is getting married?'

'Yes.'

'Ah, we have waited a long time to hear this.'

'What did you say? That Affiye is getting married?

'Yes.'

'Ancestors, thank you.'

'G-i-r-l, you didn't say Affiye was getting married, did you now?'

'Sure.'

'Get out of here, Johnson.'

'Is Affiye really, really, getting married today?'

'Today-today.'

'Then it will rain today.'

Affiye is getting married. Her fiancé? Absolutely perfect. Already on his way to becoming a well-known lawyer. Not only does he work with one of the oldest and most reputable firms in the city, but he had also just begun the process of establishing his own chambers when he learned, to his amazement, that he had been recommended for a position with the UN. So he and Affiye have gone through a rather nerve racking and long six months, during which he submitted all the necessary papers and even appeared for what could be described as some sort of an interview with the UN. While at the same time, the two of them wondered whether he should not ignore that opportunity and continue setting up his offices. In the end, the general view was that 'good sense has prevailed,' when he accepted the UN job and became an international civil servant. Therefore, he was in New York for a full year before he and Affiye decided to get properly married. Again because of her French, she was absolutely sure that it would not take too long before she joined him in some capacity or the other at the same revered organisation.

He is home for the wedding.

Affiye is getting married today.

And her groom? She agrees with everybody on that one. He is perfect. He has not only managed to be taller than her, a feat few men from these parts could accomplish, but in all other physical ways, he is absolutely beautiful and shockingly charismatic. In fact, on meeting him for the first time, what had immediately occurred to Affiye was that in other environments where career options are plentiful, diverse and equally valued, he would have become a highly-prized male model. Long before he could have contemplated a rather staid profession like law. Jet black skin and all. She always suspected that people expected her to feel that she was marrying a boy from the neighbourhood, because he is a Northerner, who grew up in Tamale, went to school in the North and came South only for university, law school and after. Yet, she is herself only half Northern. And otherwise born, bred and educated completely in the south, until her uncle sent for her and she went abroad. His people are Northern Christians. And to be fashionable, he has recently joined the best-known international evangelical church for the country's educated elite.

Affiye is getting married today. And even here where there is never anything like a small funeral or a tiny wedding, this wedding is big. This mega church that could clearly take in two thousand and more is fully packed, with an even bigger mob outside, some of whom have already occupied the chairs in the area set out for the reception. Affiye could not claim to know a sizeable percentage of the guests. And the only way a number of the guests could identify Affiye later was because she was wearing a wedding dress.

Affiye is getting married today. According to everybody, everything has just been fantabulous. Having built a reputation for being 'strict paa!' in the four or so years she's been back, everyone contracted to do anything in connection with the wedding knew that 'they had to be on their toes,' as she herself kept repeating. Everybody shook in the knees to do everything right including the mixed bunch of family and professional consultants who decided on the canopies; the food and the drinks; as well as the chairs, tables and the tents: whom to rent from, how many and exactly when to deliver.

Affiye is getting married today. And the wedding gown is a wondrous Alencon lace for which she had to make a couple of trips to Lome to buy the fabric and get it made. It was delivered a week ago. The cake, which was created from basic American angel food mix is a tall marvel in the shape of the Eiffel tower. It came in last night.

'Did you say the wedding cake is shaped like the Eiffel tower?'

'Definitely.'

'Do you think Bake Store Classics knew what they were doing? That they were being mischievous?'

'How could they have known? Just a coincidence maybe.'

'Hm, wonders are like babies... A few every minute.'

Affiye is getting married today. And the ceremony itself has got to its absolute climax. 'Now you may kiss the bride,' the pastor is saying. Affiye giggles. She thinks that sounds like another of those new trends that mark the present from the past for her, since she returned from Europe.

But in the past wasn't it old people who always commented on how things had changed? 'Maybe I'm getting old. Maybe I am old? Actually, how old is one supposed to feel at thirty-one?'

'It depends.'

'On what?'

'Like where you are in your life.'

'Like whether you are a man or a woman.'

Affiye can't understand why she is thinking these things just when the pastor is asking her groom to kiss her. Is it normal for people to think such things in the middle of their wedding? It probably depends. Like everything else.

Her groom must have kissed her. Although she was later to wonder whether he and the wedding guests had noticed any hesitation on her part. At first she had hoped and even prayed that they hadn't. But she was later to accept that it wouldn't have mattered anyway, considering...

Then she sees him.

It's Matty. Yes, it is Matty and not a ghost. Her grandmother was the craziest cynic she'd ever known and she had told Affiye once that there are no ghosts. And that if there are they can't do anything for us or against us. 'Ho, ghosts?' she had laughed out loud. 'What can they do? If they were strong, would they have died?' No, her grandmother was not a nuclear physicist, a post-modern anthropologist, or a social scientist and commentator. The old lady could never have written a word to save her life. In fact, the farthest she ever travelled was to Accra, to see Affiye born. After which she stayed for exactly one year looking after her and her mother. When the year was over, she returned to the north. And that was that.

So it is Matty. A thinner-than-remembered Matty. With a twinkle in his eyes and that half-smile around his mouth. It is Matty. And he is sporting a slight tan, with specks of grey in his hair. Funny, but although he is sitting way back out there on one of the plastic chairs in the last row, she is seeing him really close-up. Like through the zoom lens of a first-class camera.

And now their eyes are locking.

It has begun to rain. Heavily and furiously. With lots of thunder and lightning like some old-fashioned tropical downpour from the geography books. Affiye cannot tell whether the water running down her face is her tears, or from the rain. In these parts and in these droughty days, it would not have occurred to any of the people who were in charge of hiring and setting up the canopies to check them for tears and other holes. Now she can't tell what all the commotion and screaming is about. And whether the extremely loud babbles of the guests are from the horror and their consternation at the rain or her behaviour... But what the hell does it matter anyway? It is never going to be clear to anybody or even to herself, whether as she is swaying gently backwards, she is actually passing out or not... In any case, she is never ever going to remember how this whole incredible afternoon ended.

One or Two
Bourgeois Concerns

'Tawia.' Fii calls her full name, unusually.

In that voice, she thinks. You know, the one that belongs to the angry father, the irritated older brother, the fond lover and the misunderstood husband.

But she is ready for them all.

If the press in these parts were as keen on naming generations as the press in, say, the West, theirs would be dubbed Generation UN for Undersized Names. Consider this. As a Friday-born, of course he was automatically called Kofi from day one. Then his own mother and the rest of the family began calling him Fiifi from the moment they guessed he would answer to a name. It was then a quick hop to refer to him as Fii. Meanwhile, as 'one who followed twins' in our part of the world, the Creator had christened her Tawia. But her family and friends had always called her Taay, and now simply T.

'Yes dear?'

'You are overdressed, again,' he says.

He regrets the words immediately. Actually, it's not quite like that. He doesn't speak out the words and then regret them later. The regret is born in the same instance as the words. Gathering themselves together on his tongue, they rush out like a flash flood: capricious, dangerous and sweeping blessings out and away. But the days when such words could hurt her are long gone.

'Why are you dressed so... so... so...?'

'So what?'

'Gorgeously?' Of course he feels foolish now.

'Gorgeously?'

'Gorgeously is what I said.'

'But Fii darling, when was dressing gorgeously ever wrong?'

'I'm thinking of a word like inappropriate, or unnecessary, or too beautiful.'

She throws back her head and laughs: absolutely delighted. All tension gone.

'I mean... you are looking too beautiful for an occasion like this evening.'

'So the real problem is that you don't want me to look good for your guests?!'

They've been here before, at this same place. And they both know it. He also knows that she is deliberately misunderstanding him. What he really wants to say is what he is saying now.

'T, we are the hosts. We are in our home. We should be comfortable receiving our guests.'

'Do I look like I am uncomfortable?'

'Of course not!'

A pair of coffee-coloured trousers of a currently fashionable cut; a short-sleeved light brown shirt, the front embroidered in a delicate leafy motif, the body a neo-A-line with a deep V-neck that hints at her cleavage; are all highlighted by a pair of the most discreet gold earrings; a dozen of the thinnest bangles imaginable; her wedding and engagement bands on fingers so lovely in their slenderness and length; and with toes that bear the evidence of Lafa's impeccable manicure job.

Yes, they have definitely been here before. In the five years since they packed up and came home, they've thrown two other parties. One big affair and a much smaller close friends-and-family evening. They would like to have done more. A party a year. Both of them love going out for dinners by themselves or with friends and to parties when other people throw them. But they have had to accept that here, people hardly do. Of course, when you throw a party they come. They phone promptly and accept your invitation and then proceed to invite their friends and relatives, all the while assuring those friends and relatives that you really will not mind...

On both those two other occasions they had the same argument about the way she dressed. This evening, she has told herself that she will be calm and cool in the face of her husband's criticisms. She will maintain her collected self through the evening and see to it that she enjoys her own party. There will be plenty of time later to face the problem of how one should dress as a hostess.

Of course, she knows that a big part of Fii's worry is how he should dress to stand beside her. An issue that could be dealt with speedily by letting her help him choose his clothes. After all, she helps him select his clothes most mornings for the working day and also for going out. And he always seems to welcome her suggestions. Except on those two other pre-party occasions, when he had complained that whatever she had chosen was 'too much.' 'Too much' of what or for what, she didn't have the time or courage to work out. In any case, she knows better. Whatever she selects for herself, she looks great in. So feeling quite pleased with herself, she is giggling shamelessly. And why not? She knows that in the end, she will look more elegant than half her female guests, if not all. And in any case, it is her party... And the open admiration in the eyes of the male guests? That, strictly, is Fii's problem. She knows that nothing escapes him. He could be jealous. Too bad!

'Fii Sweetheart, you know I like to think I take trouble with my clothes...'

'Especial trouble.'

'Okay, I take ess-pecial trouble to dress nicely when I am hosting people. Because I want them to feel good. I want them to feel welcome.'

There. It's out. She says 'feel welcome' in that deep rounded way which sounds almost ritualistic, sacramental. Like a priest assuring his flock that joining him at the altar for Holy Communion was not only all right, but the stated desire of Our Lord...

So here it is. Out in the open. Although she is also amazed at how easily she has now voiced what surely must be an irrational fear about how welcome or not, she expects her guests to feel depending on what clothes she wears. He listens to her, hears her and wonders about the gravity with which she has tried to explain herself. But they have to get on with being ready. He says an okay that is a mixture of understanding and resignation. Then he moves away.

If he had not completely forgotten about the discussion the first time they'd had it, he would have tried to bring it up later for them to continue until something got properly cleared up. But he did forget about it. So it had happened a second time and the argument had ended more or less in the same way. With her carrying on with that unnatural vehemence about how she likes to take especial trouble to dress nicely when she is hosting people because she wants them to feel good... to 'feel welcome.'

He thinks it's all rather strange... and maybe just part of being female? Not that he has any clue of how it is to be female. But that should explain why he feels differently about everything. He is male... Yes, it may just be male to think that if one goes to the trouble to provide food, drinks, music, good company and all the other stuff that go into the organisation of a good party, then surely, one should feel perfectly free to dress as one likes, without worrying about the message one's clothes are sending out to the guests? He found himself thinking about all this in the middle of some night. And although at the time T was breathing softly by him, in his mind's eye, she seemed rather remote in a way that was new to him, which in turn hit him with a deep and terrifying loneliness. For some time, he lay in the darkness wondering whether to wake her up and talk to her about what he was feeling. But he dismissed the idea immediately, telling himself that even if she'd been awake, he would not have brought anything of the sort up for discussion. 'What a very odd business,' he thought. 'Maybe in the morning?' Soon he drifted off to sleep. Of course he had forgotten all about it in the morning. And in fact, he hadn't remembered anything of it the whole of that day, or ever again. Until this evening as they were getting dressed for their guests.

Tawia had wondered every now and then that perhaps if they'd lived in a place where one could easily go for psychoanalysis, she would've long ago dealt with it with some professional help. Emphasis on 'easily' and 'professional.' But here, where does one go? And to whom? Yet the good Lord knows that we could do with some professional shrink jobs: each one of us and our mothers and fathers, not to mention our cousins tenth-removed. Plus everybody else in-between. The whole nation in fact.

'Watch your mouth, lady. You are not trying to say that everyone in this entire society is mad, are you?'

'What? Me? How can I say such a thing?'

'Well...?'

'Of course not! All I wanted to say is that we could all do with some help.'

'Just watch it, please.'

'Okay... Okay... Okay!'

'In any case, what do you mean by you could have treated yourself to some analysis blah, blah, blah?'

'I'm serious.'

'I suspect you are.' He said it quietly. 'Oh yes, you are,' he repeated, even more quietly. 'That is what is so annoying about it,' he added. And he knew immediately that he had arrived at that place where he would have cried real tears, if he too had been a woman and allowed the luxury to cry. But he is a man and no you can't cry. You shouldn't. In fact, it is completely forbidden. How seriously tiring being male sometimes is, he thought ruefully. Meanwhile, she was watching him and dreading what was going to surely follow: about how if it had not been for her begging and pleading, they never would have left America and come back home...

Home?! That word should rhyme with hole.

'I am so sorry...' she said, apologetically.

'Sorry?' he shot back, his voice nakedly angry now. It was quite clear that he expected the apology. After all, she could have had any kind of analysis when they were in America. But she never once expressed any interest in it. She never even appeared to know anything about such things. And now listen to her talking about wanting something like that here, where nobody thinks you need help unless you are properly mad, chasing people with a cutlass or a hoe, or some other deadly weapon. Or, walking down the street completely naked...

Oh, just listen to Tawia. As if the crime of having dragged them home was not bad enough.

'Dear Lord, woman, be sorry all you want.' He couldn't help the disgust in his voice.

'But I am,' she pleaded, desperately. 'We can always go back.'

'Oh, yes?' he snorted. And even that was not enough to give expression to what at that point he recognised and she sensed was panic. Could she be going mad after all?

'Well, you had better not panic. Not now.' He was thinking aloud. 'Because in about two hours the guests will arrive. Or rather, two or three of them will... gatecrashers, most probably.'

For some reason, here, the only guests who are likely to show up on time are those you didn't invite. Somewhat maddening since you could not afford to invite all the other people you knew and should have asked. Now you are getting ready to greet people whose very existence you had not been aware of, showing up at your door as your guests and smiling because they had heard about the party from your sister's husband's other cousin... And they are early because what's the point in gate-crashing a party, if you are going to miss out on the major goodies? As for the invited guests, the earliest they will probably begin to appear will be two hours later. And that includes your sister and her husband. Depending on their personality, the rest will creep, crawl, or leap in between eight o'clock and midnight. For 6 pm. That is between two and six hours late.

'You are complaining? Why? *Ah woso eye dodow.* Don't you think you are fussing too much?'

Anyway, if you are well-organised hosts like T and Fii, you can always afford to have a little disagreement followed by a major tantrum, or even a nervous break-down and still recover in time to glide to the front door and greet your first gatecrashers.

It was a long time ago. Before she and Fii had met. It was at the end of her second year in America. She had just handed in her thesis and knew from her professor's attitude and comments that she would grad-uate. You know the feeling. Complete relief. You know the kind of feeling that persuades you that after this, life cannot ever again present you with any challenges you will not be able to deal with. So when Charles 'Chas' Mensah phoned her and invited her to supper at his home, she was ready. She and Chas had been good friends since they had met at the university back home: she a freshman and he a young lecturer. Chas was fun. She was not in his department and never took any of his classes. But from the comments other student friends made, she had learned that he was also fun as a lecturer. One of the few on campus who didn't act like they were gods, or, at the very least, oracles. And out of the classroom, Chas Mensah didn't behave as if talking to undergraduates was 'lowering standards.' In fact, at one time, she had heard a rumour that the Vice-Chancellor himself had called Chas and pointed out to him that he, the V-C, did not think it was seemly for Chas to be too familiar with students. 'Chas, is it true?'

She had asked him about it. 'Yes,' Chas had replied easily but briefly too.

It had been on her tongue to make some remark about old African academics whom stuffiness suited to a tee, since they seemed to model themselves on those dons of Oxford and Cambridge in far away England. But she had thought better of it and bitten her tongue. Really, she'd asked herself, what did she know about Oxford and Cambridge? Apart from the little she had read, or heard? Besides, after that very short 'yes,' Chas had not continued with that particular conversation. If anything, he had discouraged further reference to the whole business. Meanwhile, it had seemed in those days as if she was the only one in the world who believed a woman and a man could be very good friends, without ever wanting to get into bed together.

'Chas and I? There's nothing between us. Absolutely nothing.'

'Uh-huh?' Siedua snickered. Her huge eyes dancing with delighted doubt.

'We are just buddies.'

Sandoa laughed out loud and in such a way that made her signature 'Uh-huh, tell me another story' seemed unnecessary. Those were two of Tawia's closest girlfriends. It had not helped that Chas was having the same problem with his friends. His male friends had just been cruder.

By the time Chas left for the United States, she had come to accept that no one wants to handle the notion of a woman, especially a young woman, having a life independent of a man. And those who seemed convinced of that included all the adults she knew. As far as everyone was concerned, God had not meant any woman and any man to be just friends. The day came when Tawia told herself that there was absolutely no point in trying to get even her girlfriends to believe that she was not sleeping with Chas. Even when she had a 'boyfriend' they still didn't believe that she and Chas were only good friends. Besides, she also turned out to be some sort of a late starter in the falling-in-love department. In fact her girlfriends almost gave up trying to understand her relationship with males. And by the time she met Fii and could not help but behave like any fool in love, her girlfriends were not around for the drama. Meanwhile, half-playfully, like he didn't believe her either, but also seriously, like he appreciated the thought of it, Fii would say: 'Hei, that is so flattering… To think that I'm the first man you've fallen "properly" in love with. That is so heartwarming!'

By the end of Tawia's second year, Chas had won a place with a full scholarship at the University of California for his doctoral degree. Then two years after Chas left, she graduated and went to do her national service, teaching at Three Regions Secondary School. The students called the school TRESS and referred to themselves as TRESSES! Sometime during the year of her national service, the headmaster had called her to his office one late afternoon and wondered aloud as to whether she had considered staying to teach at TRESS after her service.

'No,' she had blurted out, surprised.

119

'Well, is it something you *could* consider?' he had pursued, gently. She had been openly flattered. The man was not only telling her he thought she was good enough to continue teaching in his school, but was doing it in so careful a way, you would have thought he was making her a marriage proposal or something... In the end, she had taught at TRESS for two more years. Then she too got admission and a generous scholarship to the University of California to do her Masters. Not surprisingly, Chas had had a lot to do with that. In fact, it was with his encouragement, as well as more substantial help in the form of advice on how to tackle the intricacies of the many applications that had got her through.

It was exactly four years after Chas left Ghana that Tawia flew into LA and she wasn't too surprised that he had come to the airport to meet her with a woman whom he introduced as his wife Donatta, also from Ghana and their two children: a girl and a boy. And boy, did Donatta look good! Petite and sleek like a pin, she was dressed in a perfectly coordinated set of elegant late summer casuals. Forest green pants, olive cotton crinkly blouse, forest green mules and a leather handbag that missed being a tote by an inch or two in height and width and so deep a jade, you would be forgiven for thinking it was black. In fact, in her typically warm way, she had jumped to embrace Donatta. But she had had to stop in her tracks since Donatta had stretched out a hand for her to shake. She later learned that their daughter was three years old and the son one year old. Over the next few semesters, Tawia and Chas met regularly and occasionally had lunch together at one or other of the eateries on and around campus. They never went out for supper, which was perfectly understandable. After all, he was a family man and would want to go home to his wife and children at the end of the long hours on campus.

It had never occurred to Tawia to wonder why Chas never invited her to his home. However, during those two years, she always asked Chas how Donatta was whenever they met. Chas would answer simply: 'She's fine,' or 'She is okay.' And when they parted she would say, with the polite concern of their common upbringing, 'Please greet Donatta for me.' To which he would reply, 'Sure,' or 'I will,' or 'Definitely.' Meanwhile she had not thought it odd that he never said to her: 'Oh, Donatta says hello,' or 'Donatta asked me to greet you for her.' No, she never wondered a bit, being the kind of person she was. Besides, the truth was that it was Chas who was her friend, not his wife. And since she and Donatta had never had an opportunity to build any kind of relationship in this foreign land, she had not missed her. If the thought of Donatta made Tawia nervous in any way, it was because they had not met even once since that initial meeting at the airport and she was not sure she would recognise Donatta on a chance encounter, while fearing that on the other hand, Donatta might easily recognise her. And frankly, the last thing she wanted was for Chas's wife to think she was a snob. Happily, there had been no chance encounters.

Chas had not wanted to admit to himself that his wife was not keen on them hosting Tawia either to a meal in their home or even in a restaurant. Right from the week

Tawia arrived, he'd kept making suggestions in that direction every now and then, but each time to a clearly indifferent response. Mercifully, Tawia had not been aware of any of that. Or she would have worked hard to rid him of any sense of obligation. But eventually, Chas seemed to have worn Donatta down with his persistence. He had invited Tawia to dinner at a time when she was in one of her serial unsatisfactory relationships. He was a doctoral candidate from East Africa whom she had been tempted to invite along when Chas first asked her. Chas's face lit up immediately. 'Of course, bring him!' he exclaimed without adding that he had secretly hoped to meet this latest date before he too disappeared. He had always worried about how brief each of Tawia's dating episodes were, beginning from when they were both on the campus back home and now here at UC. The male African population on campus was not any easier on her than the men at home. Just a little more careful. So once again, Tawia soon becomes famous for 'going through men as if they were Kleenex tissues,' while poor Chas felt compelled to come to her defence.

'Oh no, she is not like some man-eating vampire or anything like that…'

'Uh-huh?' a listener would mutter, clearly unconvinced.

'In fact,' Chas would bravely soldier on, 'with her it is the direct opposite. She's just into her own world.'

'And by that you mean?'

'Just that sooner or later, anyone Tawia dates gets the impression that she does not care for him at all, or not enough. Like she doesn't give a guy much attention. And we want attention, no? And if any of those guys takes it into his head to date other women to make her jealous, well they end up feeling worse, because she never shows any jealousy…'

All of this added to why Chas was so clearly disappointed when Tawia changed her mind and informed him that she was not bringing her latest guy to supper after all.

Tawia already knew from Chas that he and his wife and children lived in an apartment about four miles from the campus. She was ready when Chas came for her and since there was no reason for them to hang around her room, they went out, got into his decidedly old car and then were on the road. Soon Chas was entering the parking space for his apartment complex. He opened a front door, they went up a flight of stairs and then she and Donatta were saying 'hello'…

Then she found herself gasping and gasping and gasping, while wondering at the same time whether her hosts were noticing her reaction. Later, she was also to wonder whether her hostess's drab garb would have made such an impact on her, if there had been other guests, or even the one other guest she had decided in the end to drop. Because if there had been someone else there, she would not have been the only one to get the full impact of whatever message their hostess was trying to send. The message would have been diffused. Muted perhaps. It was even possible that with someone else around, T may not have noticed Donatta's clothes at all, or read any message from them. But there were no other guests, so she was to live to regret not taking the current boyfriend along after all.

Donatta was virtually in rags. Or what seemed to be rags. Not torn or tattered clothes, but a sad, dull, ill-fitting and faded assemblage of pieces which Tawia couldn't bring herself to describe in detail and which she read as a message from her hostess: that she didn't care what this particular guest thought of her or her clothes.

Tawia never really relaxed that evening in Chas's home. After all, she could not help wondering whether the woman she had met at the airport was the same as her hostess for the evening. To begin with, Donatta made a big show of having to divide her attention between the adult company and the children. The food was not memorable. And even if it was good, its qualities would have escaped Tawia. All she was aware of was that every morsel she tried to swallow nearly choked her. With Donatta quite pointedly refusing to join in on any topic Chas and Tawia were discussing and not bringing up anything herself, the conversation too had been a disaster. In fact, the entire occasion had been a nightmare, to be regretted over and over again, especially her decision not to bring the current boyfriend along.

She never went to Chas's home again. She was never asked back. She tried to invite them to her apartment, but Chas's response was not at all enthusiastic. It was always rather cool. Too cool in fact. They were always discussing possible dates, as if the three of them were the busiest people in the world. Or they were planning a

dinner for twenty presidents and half-a-dozen prime
ministers. And so after a while, she let the idea drop. She
could never decide whether the lack of enthusiasm was all
his own, or came as a package from him and Donatta.

So who on earth is going to tell me that I cannot
dress up for my guests and make them feel good and
make myself feel very, very good?! Not even my
darling Fii can get away with that kind of
presumption. No, not even Fii has that right…
And right now, here I am emerging from my
bedroom, pausing by the kitchen to check out
what the caterer is offering for the evening.
And thoroughly satisfied I am gliding to the porch
to greet my first guests. Gatecrashers or not,
I know that I look great…

Funny-Less

For Kinna, David and Nana Owiredu Kariara

All that was twenty-five years ago. Now here is Victoria, sleek and self-confident, a recently retired sixty-year-old woman on a decent pension from working as a civil servant. She is back here at Cape Coast for the funeral of her mother, the second of the only two people she had always known that she would have to return to these parts to bury: the father who had been bitterly driven out of her life and the mother who had tried to compensate for that crime. Right from the beginning, she had always accepted that it would fall on her to pay for every aspect of the funeral: from the coffin right down to all the real as well as the symbolic *kenkeys* that would be consumed during the entire mourning period. All manner of expensive but needless items would be purchased and entire programmes would be drawn up, mostly without her knowledge or approval and with no consideration for her spending power or plain old feelings. Everybody expects her not to mind any of this: not even the fact that so many of the bills would follow her to Hampstead later.

What she had flatly refused to do was to bring a coffin with her from England to bury that woman in. Something they thought her mother deserved and they felt the reputation of their family called for.

'Ah, she and her husband worked all those years in England. And between them, they only had those two sons to look after. What does she do with her money, eh? And we hear those children are doing very well too.'

Is this the home she had missed and dreaded to return to in equal measure?

So much has changed with time. But also, nothing has changed.

'What did you say that makes of women?'

A very ready response: 'the sauce… the soup… or the stew, even.'

'So in this system, what are men?' Victoria asks.

'Salt!' the elderly gentleman answers promptly. He is one of her uncles.

Victoria is startled, sure that she was barely halfway into the question when he responded, as thought he had anticipated it.

'Oh yes?' She could not have kept the cynical surprise out of her voice if she had tried.

'Yes.' He displayed not just confidence in the knowledge behind that piece of information but also the complete rightness of it.

The soup, the stew, the sauce, the source. Salt. Whenever she recalled the conversation in English later, she wondered about all those 'esses,' noting that they had added some extra poignancy to the exchange, as she listened in their language and also did her simultaneous translation: a habit she has acquired over the years. But then, even in their language and even without all those 'esses,' the discussion had sounded weighty enough.

'And no sauce, or soup, or stew tastes any good without salt… Is that the idea?'

'That's it.'

The first uncle pronounces this last agreement with open appreciation for her intelligence, leaving her wondering whether he thinks she should feel flattered by his attention.

'Yes,' chimes in a second male, another elderly gentleman. 'You see, you can eat any sauce or soup or stew anytime… without salt.' This is followed by a self-conscious pause. 'But you can never eat salt by itself under any circumstances.' An aunt passing by, carrying a child of about three years of age and her grandchild presumably, overhears the conversation. She stops and then finishes the statement for the last speaker with what Victoria later thinks was an unmistakably deep satisfaction.

All of this is taking place in the courtyard of the family house sometime during the final clan gathering a few days after the burial of Victoria's mother and the first funeral party, which is followed by the 'Thanksgiving' service on Sunday and then the second funeral party. There are a lot of other relatives standing around and within earshot.

So how and when did that system evolve of over-indulging both boy and girl children to their ruin, resulting in the population of so many homes with so many non-productive individuals? Could it be a tendency borne out of a mixture of over-protectiveness on the one hand and pure-and-simple guilt on the other? Victoria nearly moves to introduce these questions but stops. 'This is really, really, heavy,' she muses and finds herself wishing she were something like a sociologist, or at least, she had ready access to one these days. She concludes with an acute sense of frustration that is only tempered by the knowledge that, in a few days, she would be leaving these shores anyway and going back to an environment where no one would believe that in some other universe, some people actually find themselves asking such questions, sometimes.

Victoria catches herself again translating the exchanges into English, inconsequentially, but also as though to escape into that other, and yes, safer world, while repeating to herself: 'sauce, soup, stew… salt.' All those 'esses!' She doesn't know that she has smiled to herself, until the first uncle asks her with obvious disapproval whether she thinks anything is funny.

'No, no, no. Oh no' responds Victoria. 'It is not funny at all.' She says this rather quickly, not just because she does not want to offend. She honestly believes that nothing that has come out of those exchanges in the last days and hours is funny. Nothing.

So why is Victoria packing up to return to London with her boys after only one week back home? With her boys. Oh, definitely with the boys and away from all those people who seem to think that here too, the boys are somehow not good enough to be considered fully human? 'The wrong gender? My intelligent and hand-some sons? And in any case, isn't the whole world mad about boy children?' She kept asking herself these and other questions until she concluded that it's some kind of upside down space, the world of those Akans.

Victoria and Appo had planned to come home to set up a small business. The original idea was that she and the boys would move back to Accra for three months so that she had plenty of time to check out viable prospects. However, she had also accepted when they landed that the proper thing to do was to go straight home to Cape Coast to see her family despite the fact that Mamaa had not even waited for her plane to take off that first time she left to go to England before renting her old room out. And those tenants were not about to move out ever. So here she is in her mother's bedroom, surrounded by Mamaa, some very excited aunts and other older female relatives. Some nephews had taken the boys out to the beach.

'Vicky, all this time, I thought that your first-born was a girl.' This from Aunt Araba, who always prided herself on being outspoken.

'What?!' Victoria asked.

The room, which had been full of excited female voices, is suddenly quiet.

'Yes, o-o-o, that's what we all knew.'

'What?!'

'Yes o-o-o.'

'But… but how?' Victoria experienced a second's dizzy spell as she looked around to get the undivided attention of the gathering: 'Aunt Araba... Aunt Esi, how could that have been, when on all the occasions I phoned, I clearly told Mamaa that the baby was a boy?'

'Well,' Victoria's Aunt Araba charged on, 'I don't remember who told me, but that's what I heard.'

'Well, they were wrong,' Victoria declared emphatically, but also completely deflated, disgusted and furious.

'Well, too bad they were wrong. After all, what are we going to do with two boys?... Eh?' The speaker turned to the others for confirmation. 'Eh-heh, two boys. What are we going to do with them?'

'W-h-a-t?!' screams Victoria, not even trying to understand.

'What?!!!' she shouts, absolutely furious.

'What?!!!' she hisses with grief.

At this point, every aunt and cousin in the room finds her voice. But Victoria can only hear a repetition of 'I thought so too... I thought so too.'

'Mamaa?!' she called out to her mother who had been staring at nothing but now looks up.

'Actually, I always thought they were girls. At least, I thought one of them was,' her mother mutters.

'Mamaa?!' Victoria calls out to her mother again, but this time in a voice filled with a mixture of pain, incredulity and just plain old fatigue. She suspects that her mother had deliberately misinformed everybody about the gender of her children.

And now she could recall how Mamaa had always asked about 'the children' or 'my grandchildren:' never mentioning them by name, never referring to their gender. Which had not seemed odd at all at the time to Victoria, since like most African languages, Akan is not gender-specific beyond naming and has no genderised personal pronouns…

'Christ!' she swore.

Victoria and Appo didn't want to be like those expat characters who breezed in 'to check the situation out,' and then breezed out after two weeks and then declare to the whole world that they can't go back home because 'things don't work out there' and the way they see it, 'things don't look like they'll work out there in the next fifty years, blah, blah, blah.' She and Appo had wanted to give the entire project their very best shot. So that if 'things' did not work out anyway, it would not be because they gave up too soon. In any case, they had gone into the project with a failure-is-not-an-option attitude. So right from the beginning, they had planned it carefully. Very, very carefully. They would collapse their savings or talk to their bankers about the possibility of a loan, or raising a mortgage if necessary.

Then there was the research. They had sought out and talked to people they knew first hand, as well as others to whom they had been introduced. Couples like themselves; old schoolmates who had lived, or still lived in London, and other overseas places; people who had made the same kind of decision: to move back home to live. Some of them had set up their own successful consultancies and businesses. Victoria and Appo had told themselves that being idealistic was not going to be good enough. After all, they had two growing children to take care of. In fact, one of the conditions they'd set themselves was that they would find 'good schools' for the boys. 'Good schools? How many will you need?' One of the people they'd consulted had asked with amusement and a slight cynical edge to his voice. When both of them looked at him in confusion, he'd added that 'actually, there are plenty of good schools, except that they don't come cheap.' He then rushed to assure them that he'd said that not to discourage them, but just so they'd know. Victoria and Appo had glanced at one another, as each made a mental note to bring that matter too up for discussion later.

That's how they came to ask one of his Accra cousins to find a school for the boys for those three months they had planned for them to be in the country. In fact they had hoped that if things looked like they would work out, they would just have them stay in Ghana to continue in whichever school, even through the period Victoria would have to return to London to pack up.

'Vicky, when you arrived, you told us that you were here to stay for at least three months. And now you are packing to leave and it's not even one week. Why?' For an answer, the speaker only got silence from her daughter. 'Victoria, why are you doing this?' The daughter continued to ignore her mother. Victoria couldn't have opened her mouth to speak even if she'd wanted to. After all, not only did she have a plane to catch, she also had a serious conversation going on in her head at the same time.

'Is this woman my mother?' Without moving her lips, Victoria found herself asking the same question from

134

across the years and from different encounters with the older woman sitting on the bed. 'Really?' She asked herself again and then chuckled.

'Are you laughing at me?' Mamaa asked, unable to suppress her frustration and now also anger. This time, Victoria answered her with a simple 'no' and continued with her packing.

One early morning before leaving, Victoria awoke from a broken night with her head full of questions.

Didn't much of the known universe consider girl babies the 'wrong gender'?

Didn't much of the known universe worship boy children?

Either way, isn't it a crying shame? An outrage? A tragedy?

So why hadn't I dealt with such a monstrous issue before?

Before when?

Before what?

Do normal people begin to question their societies unless and until they have to?

Unless they are touched, one way or another?

No. We are not talking about writers and sundry agitators: they don't count.

Those were miserable days between arriving back in Ghana and leaving again for London. She knew that if she'd been of the weeping kind, she would have wept most days and never stopped. Actually, the tears were not running down her face, but she was crying all the same. Depression came to camp in her mind. What she is thankful to the Good Lord for is that they are not back in London. Because back there, if the boys were not in school or at day care, they were with her, noticing her mood changes and raining one-hundred-per-minute questions on her.

Here in Cape Coast, the boys' lives were completely absorbed in the lives of their uncles, aunts and especially cousins. Yet still there is one persistent question from her older son she hasn't been able to escape from. Why must they return home to London so soon? And the child is right. After all, before they left London, she and Appo had taken pains to get the boys to accept that they would be away for all of the summer vacation and possibly longer. So, although she had prepared for it, or thought she had, once the child asks the question, she found herself with no easy explanation to give him. Daddy had phoned to ask them to go home as soon as possible. 'But why, Mummy?' The boy pursued. And since the one thing she couldn't come out with is the truth, she offers some formula that had worked a couple of times before. 'Grown-up stuff,' she said easily, but also rather guiltily. And thinking all the while, 'if you can't convince yourself, how can you convince anyone else?' knowing children to be the worst sceptics in the world. Victoria was thinking all that as her son looked at her with eyes clearly asking whether she thinks he was a child or what?

So that she wouldn't go crazy, Victoria told herself that growing up a girl among these people was precisely why being a girl hadn't been a problem for her... All that business about every girl being a princess and every woman being a queen of her house. No, it had not been a hassle, at least not beyond the occasional person yelling at you that as a girl you must not climb trees. She was to learn soon enough that being a girl among most people on this earth is no joke. The tales her classmates and other girls had to tell! But then what did her people want her to feel, think, or do about raising children who would be regarded as less than human because they were boys? If this was the trade off, then there surely is a very big problem here too. Most definitely...

She kept pacing the floors and throwing questions at the night. Even when she did not need to, she would go to the bathroom that she shares with the younger members of the household and her two sons. Then she would return to the bedroom and sit on the bed. Meanwhile, she disapproves of the sleeplessness and the pacing around and actively hoped that no one would hear her, especially the children. After asking herself several times what was the use in lying down if she cannot sleep, she eventually lies down anyway and discovers a couple of hours later that, in fact, she did sleep: if not much, or too well. During these nights some other treacherous thoughts invaded her waking hours. For instance, that she was enjoying the solitude of sleeping alone. Without Appo, or her children.

Sooner or later, Victoria has to tell Appo about the decision to return so abruptly to London. Although she thinks she has pulled herself together sufficiently to phone, it is another story altogether when she actually tries to. As though putting into practice some stress-releasing technique she had got out of a class or a manual, she sits herself down and then breathes in and out at least half-a-dozen times before dialling. When Appo answers, she forgets to ask him how he is and just blurts out: 'I'm coming home next week with the boys.' Absolutely shocked, Appo shoots back 'why?' After the briefest pause, he hisses into the phone: 'Coming back home? But you are home?' That last statement hits Victoria so hard it stops her from breathing for a second. However, frightened of what she is going to say next and how she is going to say it, she switches off the phone to buy the minute or two she knows it will take Appo to call her back. She was later to tell him that the line was cut (since call connections do get cut in that part of the world), a lie she knows is quite unnecessary, even as she is telling it. And sure enough, the minute she switches the phone back on Appo calls back with all the questions she'd anticipated he would ask: half of which she does not have coherent answers to, or any answer at all. The rest of her responses are just incoherent monosyllables full of panic and misery.

'I'll explain everything when I get there,' she offers.

'Are you and the boys okay?' he asks again and again.

'Fine, fine… okay.'

'Really?' he pursues.

'Oh yes, yeah… perfect.'

She switches the phone off again and this time lets it stay off. For the rest of the day Appo had tried to reach her but couldn't. In desperation, he contacted his younger brother, a university student, to go and check up on her and call him back. So in the end, it is this young man who organises their return trip: calling up the airlines, which were adamant that since discounted, their tickets are now forfeit and new ones have to be purchased. Since she had not told them that they would be leaving, it had not been necessary for Victoria to stop her mother or any other relative from coming to see them off. Some of them had guessed what she was planning, but they had no idea of the specific time she was leaving for the airport.

Now safely buckled into her seat, she is sure of only one thing as the plane takes off: she is never going to come back home, if this was home. Maybe she would return to visit sometime if she absolutely had to. As for the boys, she is not going to tell them anything just yet. She will wait until they hit their teens. Then she will sit them down one day and explain everything to them. Like why some of their friends visited Ghana regularly for the holidays, but they never went. And hopefully, she would be able to do all that without them feeling bewildered. She is not going to indoctrinate them against Ghana. Oh no. In fact, she would take pains to tell them what a beautiful country it is and how wonderful and warm its people are. And if one or both of them ever wanted to go and visit, she would not do anything to discourage them. Rather she would say it is a wonderful idea and she would do all she could... then she stopped herself, knowing she was running too fast ahead of herself.

Of course Appo is at the other end to meet Victoria and their children with his normal show of affection and nine hundred kilometres of questions, all of which he had tried to ask at once and to each of which he had expected an immediate answer. But she looks knowingly at the boys and puts a finger on her closed lips. Of course, he got the message immediately, although that also had him feeling more and more curious.

It is not just in Appo's voice. His face, indeed, his whole body was one big question. Consequently the two adults became uncomfortably quiet from the moment they pulled out of the car park. During that long ride, what saves the situation are the boys chattering to themselves and commenting on the scenes that whisked past. Each of them bombarding their father with so many questions you would think it is their father who has just returned from a trip and he's been gone for years instead of just one week. Meanwhile, the father is trying to get in his own questions because he is genuinely interested in how they were and what they had been up to when they were in Ghana. And those boisterous and highly articulate boys did not disappoint. They had so many stories to tell about the numerous cousins they had met, boys and girls, as well as several uncles who had made such a great deal of fuss over them. There are stories about how the house in Cape Coast actually stands on the sea shore and how hot the sea water is and so great for swimming...

'Swimming?' their father asks, genuinely intrigued.

'Yes Daddy,' the two confirm in unison.

'Really?' The father is now perplexed, wondering whether eight days weren't rather short for preparing anybody, not to mention children, for swimming in the Atlantic Ocean. He glances at their mother who is now laughing because she'd read his thoughts and with a lot of relief that there was actually something to laugh about.

'I don't think they did any real swimming. Splashing at the water's edge and playing beach soccer under the coconut trees sounds more like it,' she assures him and almost adds that in any case, the fact that they are back here in London means that they have obviously survived whatever they did back in Cape Coast. But she doesn't add that bit because she doesn't want to make him feel foolish and in any case, any further discussion of the details might throw them into some deeper and more controversial regions.

In fact, Victoria had already noted with some concern that one or two of the questions Appo is asking the boys are part of his sly attempt to get some idea of why they are back here already which made her not a little jittery. However, since she cannot ask him not to talk to them, she continues to sit on the edge of her seat, literally shaking at the thought that everything can come out any minute. Actually, she has completely overlooked the fact that there is no way anything 'could come out,' since the boys did not know anything anyway. But yes, she is going to tell Appo everything.

Mixed Messages

'Quaaba.'

I am startled.

'Quaaba my Precious, I have told you over and over and over again. As a member of the *Nsona* clan, even the back of your head is prettier than someone's face.' I am twelve years old.

Nana had caught me at it again. Studying my face and finding every single feature on it wanting. Sometimes actually talking to myself or to my image in the mirror. She never tired of catching me. Not after she realised – and I never knew when that was – that anytime I was not in school, or sitting by the grand table in the hall doing my homework, or she just did not see me around, or on any of the zillions of errands she always sent me on (the only reason adults have children in Africa is to send them on errands), I would be in the room I shared with my two cousins, staring at my face and thinking myself ugly. Nana's point was that I should relax: there was nothing wrong with my face.

Well, I thought she should relax and give all those assurances a break. After all it was just my face. I mean it was only my face I was worried about. No, the rest of me was okay. In fact, not just okay, but perfect. Thanks to Nana and everybody else around me when I was growing up, I was convinced that I had the perfect body.

I had a great pair of butts, which meant big. Not necessarily huge, but big and rounded enough for them to wobble behind me as I walked. As far as my grandmother and her age mates were concerned my butts stood out like the two solid supports they should be: for my backbone, my hips, my thighs, my legs. If anybody tried to correct Nana that it was rather the other way, that hips, thighs and legs supported butts, she would question, 'what are you saying?' Any attempt to explain and she would stop the discussion with: 'Well, solid buttocks are part of solid hips. And together they give a solid character to the thighs, the legs and even the feet.' The notion of me and my ideal body but imperfect face followed me through adolescence. They also told me I had the proper height for a woman, whatever that was.

Yet, from the moment I first stepped off the plane in Europe and throughout my many years' sojourn here in North America, it was not my face that got me into trouble. I have had to squeeze what have turned out to be my unacceptably large bottoms into all manner of corsets and girdles and body shapers. Clearly, out here, I am one of the women for whom spandex was invented, while also learning quite early that nothing that has or ever will be created could ever re-engineer my body to give me that 'dream shape to die for.' A shape the retailers of those body-moulders proclaimed could be mine in the advertising fliers that were never missing from my junk mail wherever I have lived in America, be it Richmond, Los Angeles, Seattle, Cincinnati or New York City.

'*To whom to,*
To whom to
To whom do these ntumbor akese belong?'

They definitely were the same butts to whose movements my male colleagues (including some in the Socialist Alliance!) used to beat rhythms in *sotto voce* behind me. When I caught them at it, they would quickly assure me that they had not sung any such song, but still thought that socialist or not, and brilliant mathematician or not, my backside was uniquely... ehem, ehem, 'Sisterhood, we are sorry o, but not really too sorry.'

'Ugh, that was terrible,' offered Pamela.

'It was.' That was me, decades later in the Bronx.

'I hope you didn't think it was just funny, or in any way okay?' Joscalynn added, her voice steely with a sense of outrage.

'No, I didn't think so.' I said that very quietly, not at all sure what I'd felt then.

'You should have sued them,' Julie added.

'Sued them?' Me again, intrigued and nearly adding, 'whom?' but luckily remembering in time where I was and therefore saying rather stupidly, 'oh yes, I should have sued them.' And not adding, 'if it had been here and these days,' because in those days and even here, one would not have thought of suing. As for out there at home, not only would it have been out of the question then, but no one thinks of such things even now.

Or medical malpractice. Why, everybody knows the hospital knew that my cousin died from a transfusion with blood that was not only contaminated but actually stank – that's what Uncle Kofi alleged anyway – yet what the family began to worry about during the three weeks my cousin Dee was in a coma was what kind of coffin to bury her in and whether it should be in Mankessim where she had been born and had grown up but was 'only her father's place' or at Nkwanta her mother's birthplace and therefore her 'proper' home and as befitted a princess of her house, although her mother hadn't lived in that village in over thirty years and Dee not at all. Naturally, the moment she actually stopped breathing, they all began to wail, and wail and wail...

'Ei, you, Quaaba, so what else do you want God to do for you?' This from my girlfriends back at home years earlier when I must have been whining again about some less than perfect facial feature.

'Look at your buttocks...'

'... And your breasts.'

'That's your cocoa farm, Quaaba.'

'Your gold mine.'

'Charley, this body of yours is your passport, o-o...!'

'...With permanent residence visas to England, Germany and Japan already stamped in...'

'...US Green Card affixed.'

'You can pick and choose, Girl.'

Yet here, it was the shape of my body that nearly sent me into therapy.

'Quaaba, please be careful.' This from Julie again.

'Why?' I asked her, genuinely perplexed by her attitude, since I'd heard that therapy or analysis does you no end of good.

'My dear, therapy is like comedy. It doesn't travel too well,' Pamela responded immediately. She of the quick wit. At which of course we all roared. The other girls agreed readily with her, as if each of them had already dealt with this issue in some earlier context. But then the point had been well-made for me too, so that although it must have taken me a full minute to nod my head or grunt agreement at the time, I never sought any therapy.

Bola Ogunmola and I had met at an African students' party. Julianne Beaufort and Joscalynn Mitchell had gone to the same grade school in Detroit where Julie's father had been a worker at Ford Motors. Pamela John and Sandra Greenley had been introduced at some must-be-there cocktail party for sophisticated American and global professionals in Lower Manhattan.

In retrospect, how we all then melded into our group of six must be one of the great cosmopolitan epics of our time. But we did meld. And from a certain point in time began to meet regularly to hang out even when we were not all exactly living in the city. As for what we did by way of earning a living, that too, was quite diverse. After my Masters, I went into high school teaching. Bola is an anthropologist and she's been in a couple of really interesting jobs, I tell you!

'Like what?'

'Like… almost like espionage.'

'Are you serious?'

'Yes.'

'For whom?'

'Mostly governments…'

'No!…'

'Shh…'

Julie became an attorney. Pamela is in city government. Joscalynn – ('not Josh, Josie, Lynn or any other pet abbreviation please.' She is firm about that. Secretly to myself though, she's always been Josca. After all, Joscalynn is too long…) – yes, Joscalynn works in a nationwide estate agency and harbours ambitions of going solo one day. In the meantime, she does moan a bit about how the banks refuse to lend her starter cash.

The youngest of us is Sandra, married with twins and the only one whose spouse's spirit has definitely always been a member of our group. A fully qualified structural engineer herself, she took the top honours in her final year. But Sandra decided to be a housewife and a stay-at-home mom 'and very proud of it too.' Sandra cannot open her mouth without mentioning her husband. We know that Robin is in accountancy and a consultant with the international branch of some really fancy financial firm:

'The only black in a senior position…'

'Oh, and at Yale, he was the only black in his class…'

'Robin is – *still is* – a Rhodes Scholar and the only person of African descent in his year…?'

'Robin is a vegetarian. He is actually vegan, the first real one in his family…'

'Robin…'

'And Robin…'

'Robin…'

'Robin…'

Even now I can swear on my Nana's grave – *mara mondue!* – that the original idea was never to meet and deal with weight matters or dieting. We did not even have a formal agenda in those days. We just got together every now and then from different New York boroughs and hung out innocently, with a few guilty pleasures. Meet at a teahouse and indulge ourselves with pieces of cake or some pastry apiece. Or for supper at some fancy eatery downtown, accompanied by a glass or two of wine. The venue varied. We also met in cafés, regular restaurants and one another's apartments, depending on who felt like hosting. 'No pressure girls' was a regular chorus in those days. And it referred to volunteering to host or not; to selections of food or drink; suggestions that we could also meet to do culture or something even more useful like volunteering. Time? Certainly 'no pressure girls' to stay longer anytime anywhere with the group than your personal plans allowed.

Sandra hosting us every month happened naturally. It was after the first two years of us as a group. Bless the dear child's heart. She is at this moment in her kitchen, out of earshot and preparing something for us to munch and crunch. Both Bola and I had graduated, but like Julie and Pam and Joscalynn, I had decided that I was severely allergic to home-making of any kind. Bola adored the idea of a home, loved to cook enormous pots of lovely food, wouldn't mind grocery shopping and going to the market and all that. But the home obviously had to come with a husband…

Oh, she got her wish all right. We met recently at a conference and my Bola looked very well. Which for us West Africans still means with her body a little above our ideal clinical weight, as by age, height, etcetera. Happy? Possibly. In any case, Bola had always insisted, the excellent sociologist she is, that 'you can't plan for happiness.' So hei…

It started quite harmlessly enough sometime after meeting at Sandra's had become the regular thing to do. For one, she not only made us feel really welcome, but very comfortable too. We could relax in a way we couldn't in any public place like a teahouse or a restaurant. We always knew we could take our shoes off and put our feet up, literally and figuratively. And we did. In fact, every now and then, it became a childish game we played: which one of us could grab that particularly comfortable sofa first. The one in the far left corner from the door with its many beautiful assortment of international throws: one woven wonder each from central and southern Africa, an *adire*, one *adinkra*, some *afghans* and a cashmere. Plus plenty of stuff to eat and drink too. So that from the sofa, and snuggled inside those priceless fabrics, you could stretch out, shut your smog-ravaged eyes and even doze off to the babble of friendly voices.

It was on one such afternoon that Pamela commented on the fact that Joscalynn was looking 'gorgeous.'

'Sweetheart it's this heavenly diet,' Josca had said.

'A new one?' the rest of us had chorused.

'The best yet.'

Joscalynn knew what she was doing. Or I hope she did, because we got hooked. What we had all overlooked was that Josca was the naturally thin one among us. She was also the one who researched new diets, tried each of them and brought us both the news and also the results on her body. For her, every new diet was 'absolutely fantastic' until the next one. She always had these 'ten pounds' she 'had to lose.' Said as though the pounds were English sterling, so this was quite a perverse and ritualistic desire to plan to lose them. We didn't know at the time that it was going to happen. But it did. From that moment, our group changed. For the rest of that afternoon and after weight loss, weight gain and diets took centre stage. We couldn't get off them.

Getting together was no longer that benign. Our meetings stopped being random. They became regular and formal. Once we were all in, no matter how hard we tried to do our regular chit-chat like earlier times, soon everyone wanted to hurry on to the crucial business of our weight. Who had lost any, how much, how and who had gained any, how much and why. Then we would start the weighing-in barefoot but in our street clothes of course. After much discussion, we had earlier agreed that each of us would subtract ten generous pounds of weight for our clothing. Did any of us try to cheat by dressing rather lightly even when it was bitterly cold outside? You bet. Silk and rayon, voile, muslin and luminex. But then reinforced with jackets and coats made of the warmest and heaviest wearable materials available.

Those of us who had lost anything from five ounces to five pounds during the past week were openly triumphant. Not only did we gloat, but we also had the extra pleasure of comforting anyone who had gained. That's the only time during those sessions when once again we could be at our supportive, sisterly best. Suddenly wise and practical, we were full of new and helpful suggestions. Or what we thought were new and helpful suggestions. In the meantime, our chorus of 'no pressure girls' had disappeared. It went, never to return. That's where we were when we found ourselves in Sandra's living room towards the end of the year 1999. It was December 16 and already very cold outside. No snow yet though. The last to enter was Julie who, after she had shorn herself of all that extra clothing, stood there, absolutely golden and gorgeous and smiling at all of us with those flirting eyes of hers.

In fact, it was not only Julie who was glowing. We all seemed to have had an excellent year and it showed all over our bodies – luminous skins and dancing eyes. Even our hairs had benefited: permed, extended, corn-rowed or close-cropped. There had been promotions for both

Julie and Robin from the beginning of September. Joscalynn and her partner had finally secured a mortgage for their dream house after some initial disappointments, despite her being in the industry and all. Bola and Chukwu were going back home. Bola had resigned from her old job and then connected with an international non-governmental organisation with a West African sub-regional office in Abuja, while Chukwu seemed to have secured an excellent position as the economic adviser to some state governor. They had actually packed up. I was going home just for a visit, as I'd been doing every two years for the longest time. And so was Pam. She was going home to Trinidad. By the way, Pam had come into quite a bit of money from the estate of a nineteenth century slave-owning English planter. Long story that. A very long story.

'Guys, this is going to be our last session before splitting for the end of the year and the New Year holidays,' Joscalynn announced, as if we needed reminding.

'Say Christmas and New Year!' That from Sandra. If Bola felt funny she didn't fess up. But I had known for a long time that at least one of her parents was Muslim.

'Anyway, let's hope we survive all these doomsday predictions,' said someone quite seriously. It could have been Julie.

'Oh that!' squashed another.

'But a few of the predictors seem to know what they are talking about,' I offered.

'Listen children,' it had to be Pamela who was calling us to order. 'People have always predicted the end of the world. And they always knew what they were talking about. But we are still here.'

No one could argue with the very sane and practical Ms. Pamela John.

Sandra was staying put, as usual, adding as a reminder that her home was New York because that's where her husband and children are and she was not going anywhere for nothing. A little too aggressive a response for us perhaps, her own sisters, and no doubt leaving us all thinking that 'there goes our Sandra again and her caginess about her parents and her original home.' Sandra nearly had us believe that she was from 'the Islands' until Pam got interested and accidentally put a little pin in that balloon. Not from any malice mind you. Pam, a Trinidadian herself, had just been curious about where in the Caribbean our little sister claimed to hail from. But Sandra had refused to be specific. Later, she made our group a peace offering by dropping her fake Jamaican accent. End of story, Sandra wished. Actually, Bola and I later did a bit of digging. What we came out with, if it was the truth, was not even that terrible. Sandra's grandfather had been a minister in one of those post-independence English-speaking African countries. So of course her father had been educated in England or the USA or Canada and he had stayed in Europe or North America all his working life. And the parental home, if it still existed, was in one of those countries. But hei, she should know that; that's her own business.

Of the other four Julie was the one I had known the longest and was closest to. She and I had been friends

154

since my first year in graduate school, since when we'd
been so close that over the years each of us had been
living quite a bit of the other's life. She had always
insisted that since my family was 'way out there in
Africa,' I should go spend my holidays with her and her
people in New Orleans. And I suspect that no invitation
of the kind had ever been so enthusiastically accepted and
so often exploited. I never seemed to have missed a single
Thanksgiving or Christmas my first half-decade here. It
was a special treat, being in New Orleans with Julie and
her people. New Orleans with its waters: Lake Pont-
chartrain and its incredible Causeway; the Mississippi
River, which I'd heard so much about while in school at
home because of how important it had been during
slavery and in spite of which I'd developed some deep and
silly affection for. Finally, as always and very specially, the
comforting feeling that the sea was out there, all around
and not too far.

New Orleans was not home. But then everything
about and around it reminded me so much of home
that going there with Julie had an effect on me that was
quite different from what I suspect she thought the
trips did for me. I always became one ball of homesickness from the moment I landed at the airport, until
I took off again for wherever I would be returning to.
The times I was at the actual family gathering were the
worst. The warm and cozy feeling of not just family,
but big family; the laughter and the food often
reminded me of home and I would feel really tummy
sick with homesickness. Of course I never told Julie

about any of this. Additional self-torture it may have been, but it never crossed my mind to give up those trips either.

Not the summers though. Being in New Orleans in the summer was not fun, since for me there is nothing that special about hot and humid coastal towns – a prominent feature of all the places I'd known as 'home' back at home: Cape Coast and Elmina, Sekondi-Takoradi and even Accra. I could also never really enter into all that local and national la-de-la about the city of New Orleans: Bourbon Street, Mardi Gras and all that. The food is of course another matter.

The rest of the group knew that Julie went south to Louisiana to be with her folks for the holidays whenever she could and quite often with me tagging along. Meeting her there for Thanksgiving was like normal and this year was no exception. There was nothing odd about the question. Although for the life of me, I have never been able to remember which of them opened her big mouth and asked it. The question was not where she was going for the coming Christmas holidays, but 'how Thanksgiving had gone.' At that Julie quite simply crumbled, completely, horribly. It was a cleaner collapse than any a demolition artist would have been proud of. First she gasped, then she gagged. Next she exhaled. After that we saw these two huge tears starting to flow from her eyes. All along, the rest of us watched her in horrified silence. But when we noticed that she was swaying slightly, we swung into action.

'What's wrong, Julie?'

'They won't... they won't... they won't let me eat anything.'

'What? At Thanksgiving with your family?'

'They won't... they won't... they won't let me eat anything,' she repeated.

'What's that Julie?'

'They won't let me eat... they won't let me eat
anything!,' she screamed through her tears.

Clearly, poor Julie was not making sense.

'Darling, don't breathe another word,' someone
pleaded. Then Sandra emerged from somewhere inside
her house, clutching a real brandy glass full of what, if we
knew anything about Sandra's taste in liquor, must have
been the most matured of some of the world's best cognac.
Although at the time, the quality of what was in the glass
was not what concerned us, since for our purpose, the
crudest hooch, or *akpeteshie*, would have done just as well.

We poured the contents of that huge glass vase
between her teeth and down her throat. She choked
again, coughing out quite a bit of the liquor in the
process. The pupils of her eyes almost disappeared and
then we heard what sounded like a death rattle coming
from her chest. Sandra now brought a tall glass of water,
which Julie rescued from our hands once she realised we
were going to force that too down her throat. She meekly
gulped it all down. That seemed to have helped. But she
was sweating profusely and someone was unbuttoning
her shirt. We half-carried and half-dragged her to
Sandra's bedroom, stripped her to her panties, put a loose
nightie that Sandra gave us on her and got her to lie

down. She must have fallen asleep immediately. While Julie slept, we discussed what we'd seen and what we thought it must have been all about.

'Guys, guys, if I'm right, I know the story,' I blurted out. The four of them turned sharply to look at me, fully in the face.

'Quaaba, you know which story?' Pam asked.

'What just happened to Julie,' I said.

'And what's that?' Pam's voice was thick with hostility. She was the one who had spoken. But she was not alone. I began to think that owning up to some knowledge about what had hurt our friend was perhaps a mistake? From my friends' reactions it looked like what I'd done was no different from confessing that I'd been an accomplice.

'Pam, please don't sound like that,' Joscalynn pleaded on my behalf.

'Okay, okay. So what's it?" prompted Bola.

'It's a long story,' I squeaked.

'It always is, isn't it?' Sandra added her voice to the inquiry.

'See, everyone in her family is like a model,' I began.

'What?' wondered Bola again.

'What's that?' Sandra screamed.

'Quaaba, what on earth are you talking about?' Pam asked.

'Folks, please. Please!' This time I had to do my own pleading. I also wanted to give them a couple of African proverbs. Or at least, one proverb in an Anglo-Saxon translation that would be intelligible to them: like *if someone is baking you a whole cake, you don't lick what's left in the mixing bowl.* But this was no time to confuse my friends with wise words from the Motherland. In any case, anytime I'd tried the proverb thing Bola had looked at me very strangely, as though wanting to ask if I knew what I was doing. So I just continued with my main narrative.

'Yes, like I said, most of the women in Julie's family are like models, gliders on the catwalk. Maybe not so tall, but definitely that thin.'

'Uh-huh?'

'Except that unlike models, who we hear don't eat, Julie's people eat. And very well.'

'All that good Creole food,' someone groaned.

'Have you ever heard of people who can eat anything they want – how much they want – anytime they want but never put on an extra ounce? Always looking like forest bamboos or beanpoles, with tummies that are flatter than grasshoppers?'

'That's not fair,' was the chorus of protest from all four. As if they'd rehearsed it.

'Not many. But they do exist,' Bola offered.

'That's Julie's people… Except Julie of course,' I said.

'Uh-huh?' someone queried again.

'But Julie is not that fat!' More protests.

'Of course not,' I agreed with them. 'Certainly where I come from,' I even added half-truthfully, 'some relation would have always tried to fatten Julie up some more.'

'Yah-yah,' assents all round. After all, who among us that afternoon would not have loved to have her own fattening kin?

'But here, things are quite different,' I continued.

'You bet!' Another chorus.

'And it seems as if Julie's people have made her aware of her body's tendency to go against the family grain and put on weight whenever possible. So much so that she has almost become afraid of food.'

'R-i-g-h-t,' someone said uncertainly. Immediately reminding us that, in fact, going back to even those long ago and far away happy days of 'no pressure girls,' it was Julie who had been more consistently aware of the fattening dangers inherent in sugars, fats and all good food and great drinks.

'Yes,' I continued 'And Julie's people know how to pig out. At least from the times I've been with them.'

'All that good Creole food!' Bola or someone else groaned again.

'The gumbos, the jambalayas, mmm!' Pam added, with all of us beginning to salivate.

'Crawfish boulettes.' That was Joscalynn.

'Stuffed crabs,' I added. Being one of those foods I'd casually concluded were directly from Africa: a heavenly but rather difficult and complicated recipe that I'd heard had been a favourite of our royalty back home, but which no one seems to be able to afford any longer and had not been cooked in nearly a century.

'Mmm, those Cajun goodies,' Pamela murmured.

'Turduckens…,' added Joscalynn.

'And Turducken rolls…,' Sandra said.

'Crawfish pies…,' Bola breathed.

'With lime ice. Mmm!'

Mixed Messages

'Or better still, mint julep…'
'Stop it!!!' Five voices screamed in desperation.

Everyone called Julie's grandmother Gromere. Earlier, it had been Gromere who had supervised the cooking for occasions like Thanksgiving and Christmas. Especially the huge turkey, which was always the centrepiece and her version of Creole ham smothered in bourbon pecan sauce. Grand, delicious and very special. Those and what she described as her 'basics' were Gromere's responsibility well into her eighties.

The year she turned ninety, Julie's mother (being the oldest daughter) repeated her standing offer to do the bird and the ham. As usual, Gromere haughtily forbade her to utter such words. This time, though, Julie's mother just said no. For once, the old lady had to shut up and listen to someone else ordering her around her own house and commanding her not to step near her own stove. Everyone within earshot froze at such audacity. But there was also secret relief, as they all remembered hearing about some half-a-dozen or so burnt-out meals and a couple of minor fire explosions. Thank God that nothing had ended up being too catastrophic. Anyhow, Gromere's response was to declare that Marie was cursing her with death. After which declaration she took to her bed and sulked until the afternoon of Thanksgiving or Christmas, when she appeared all dolled up and chirpy to take her place at the head of the table. 'Marie,' she insisted, 'you should dish out, since, my dear, you did the cooking.' Nothing about being too frail to want to do the honours.

Gromere had moved on one rule for both Christmas

161

and Thanksgiving. There should be more than enough for everybody to eat, never mind how many family members turned up for the occasion. As in any number from thirty upwards, which number was also only about half of the possible whole and made up of at least four generations. Quite often the younger generation resisted turning up for both occasions. They were only one month apart and bless their money-conscious hearts, it was incredibly expensive to do both. The attitude and the no-shows made Gromere quite unhappy. But she couldn't do anything about it. People would incessantly phone and later email and text, to make sure who would pitch up, who wouldn't and for which occasion. Whoever went for Thanksgiving, needn't try for Christmas. And vice versa.

Apart from Gromere's turkey, which was always stuffed to the nines and the ham, there would be pots and bowls and trays of all manner of cooked yummies. Meanwhile, it was also assumed that every homemaking adult – i.e. *female* adult – should bring something. That included in-laws. So the women brought loads of stuff, although it seemed to suit Gromere to think that no one ever would. Therefore, apart from the banquet that she described as her 'basics,' you can just imagine the amount of food that would be available for consumption... Normally two, three, or sometimes four kinds each of fried chicken, roasted ham, barbecued steaks, barbecued chicken, hamburgers, white fish in cheese sauce, fried catfish, trotters in gravy and yards of sauced ribs. And every year, without fail, were those very special hot and spicy Creole sausages made for Gromere by her neighbourhood butcher of some forty years.

There were ordinary hotdogs, hamburger patties and bolognas too. And bread; small dinner rolls, fat burger buns and of course, slices of different Wonder and Pumpernickels. There were different types of rice, candied yams, baked beans and corn bread. In addition, there were so many potato salads, many more lasagnas and other pasta dishes. The desserts were equally varied and numerous – cakes, pecan and other pies, ice-creams: ten or so different flavours of the latter. And if on such special occasions the old dining table groaned under the weight of all that wonderful and 'Thank-you-Lord' abundance, no one ever heard it.

So it had been a shock to me that anytime we were at these family feasts, one or other of Julie's relatives would make faces and low disapproving noises anytime Julie had more than a piece of meat or chicken plus a tuft of salad on her plate. While they heaped their plates full with chicken pieces, meats, rice, melt-in-your-mouth mashed potatoes and everything else available. Anytime Julie tried to go for seconds of anything, or pour herself some juice, pepsi or coke or any drink other than water, people would murmur under their breath, her own mother leading the charge. And desserts were completely out, including her grand-mother's really heavenly migan. In fact, the entire older generation and some of her age mates too, treated Julie like a sick person who did not know what was good for her.

This time I sensed something I should have realised before, but unfortunately hadn't. Julie never really enjoyed those family get-togethers! In fact she hated them and after a while she probably only made the effort to go down there for me 'to be with family,' since mine was 'far away in Africa.' And later, she must have gone as often as she did most certainly because of her sons. To get them not just to meet the family, but also have them integrated into it.

'Girls, it was really bad this last Thanksgiving,' I explained.

'Really?' That was from Joscalynn.

'So how come you haven't told us about it, so we would be careful?' Joscalynn again.

'But this is the first time we are together since then…' Stony faces stare at me. 'Remember Thanksgiving was only three weeks ago?' I was whining like a frustrated three-year old.

'So how bad was it?' Pamela asked with the voice of an exasperated head teacher.

'It was the worst.'

'Uh-huh?'

'Time I just told the story straight through,' I said, planning mentally to reject long interruptions. 'Julie had picked a piece of grilled chicken and a small helping of baked fish, with plain salad sprinkled with lemon. For a drink, she had poured herself a glass of diet something or other. After she'd cleared her plate, she'd asked someone to pass her a "small piece" of a family favourite: Gromere's special sausage. I clearly heard Julie say "small piece." Quicker than a lightning flash, Francie, her mother's youngest sister looked straight at Julie and said audibly: "Darling, you know you shouldn't?"'

'No, no, no!' a chorus from the sisters.

'Yes, her mother's youngest sister, her mother being the oldest, followed by two uncles, and then the two aunts…'

'No, no, no?!'

'Oh yes.'

'Unbelievable.'

'It happened.'

'Not really?'

'Yes too.'

'Gross.'

'More than gross. Outrageous.'

'So what happened next?'

'Julie just stood up and of course, so did I. Then I found myself following her out. From then on, it seemed quite natural that we should call a cab and go back to the hotel where we always stayed whenever we were in the city. By then I could understand why Julie insisted that we paid good money to hotels instead of going to stay in her beautiful family house with all those empty rooms. It was also natural that without any discussion, we packed our bags, took another taxi and went straight to the airport where thankfully on Thanksgiving afternoon, airlines can rightly behave like the *tro-tros* at home in West Africa and literally send out touts to look for passengers. Getting flights out that afternoon was not a problem. Me to the west and Julie up north and all of that done in complete silence between us.'

'Dear Lord, Quaaba!'
'Good grief, Quaaba!'

'Wow, Quaaba!'
'Ah-mazing!'

The next thing anyone said, kind of sensible this time, was Joscalynn asking me if I'd spoken to Julie before the meeting. 'Yes, of course,' I answered quickly and added, maybe too quickly, 'Not about that.' In response to which the four of them exhaled.

The five of us must have sat without talking for a good twenty minutes or more after that. Then one of us made a great deal about checking out the time. Must have been Bola. Taking the cue, we all looked for our coats and jackets and scarves, got into our shoes and readied ourselves for the cold air outside. But before leaving, we wondered aloud about Julie and what we should do. First, we agreed that for the moment, she should just be left to sleep. Sandra assured us that she would take care of Julie for the rest of the evening and also see to it that she got home safely whenever she woke up and felt able to. Maybe she would even drive Julie home instead of letting her go by train. But first, she would phone Julie's boys and get some non-alarming info to them.

Then we dispersed.

So does anyone understand why barely a week later when I was back home, after thirty hours of travelling and within the first few hours of arrival, I was angry and confused that Mamaa, my mother's oldest sister, should have examined me from head to toe and asked me why, with so much food that they had heard was in America, my collar bones were all out for the world to see? 'Why,

Quaaba, why?' she repeated in case I hadn't heard her the first time, 'Why haven't you been eating?'

My aunt's first words to me in two years. I had no words to answer her. And she had not waited for any.

'Between now and when you return to America, whenever that is,' my Big Mother warned loudly, 'I am going to feed you some good palm nut soup and *fufu*, rice and stews and *banku* and okra sauces, with some fresh fish, chicken and goat and…' To show that they approved of her concern, everyone laughed: my mother the loudest.

NB. This tale is to the memory of Dr. Sylvia Ardyn Boone:

'Sylvie, we are still grieving, although we shouldn't. After all, you illumed us forever.'

Delight

For Kobby, Maa Dwowa and Precious

Torturing little frogs and toads. Chasing butterflies, sunbeams and light beams, raindrops, soap bubbles that fly slowly up and never come down, yellow flowers blooming in the wild or in a nicely cultivated garden. These and other gifts from the great outdoors get kids to jump up and down, throw out their arms and kick at nothing. They giggle, their necks flung back until those beauty folds would seem un-creased and we would wonder why we had to grow up.

But then what did I have to light up those eyes with? I, whose attempts at pots-on-the-balcony horticulture proved my thumb to be the un-greenest in the world? A recent city widow imprisoned by two arthritic knees on the third floor of an apartment building with a broken-down lift and a landlord who doesn't seem to remember ever that he has tenants until the rent is due?

I realise suddenly that one of them has shifted his attention from the rest and is looking intently at what I am doing. He is the youngest, just over two years old.

And what am I doing but working at the fruitless task of getting my once famously beautiful fingers to forget the gnarl, the wrinkles and the dryness?

When I catch his eye, first he turns away. Then he moves back to face me. Fully. Frontally. For a second, I wonder what he is going to say. But then he doesn't say anything. Just stretches his hands, both palms up. Following his eyes, I pick the bottle of white lotion, press the pump and put a dollop into each palm. He looks at the drops of lotion, his eyes growing to thrice their size, all his funny milk teeth out, then, literally drooling, he skips to show them to the others. So they too come up to me, four palms up. I drop lotions into each palm. Now it is not just six enlarged eyes, three drooling mouths, three sets of teeth all out, but also, six flaying hands, six kicking legs, plus the squeals, the squeals, the squeals...